Elizabeth's older sister?

"You're Elizabeth's sister, right?" Ethan said eagerly. "That's right!" Elizabeth smiled. "I'm Geraldine, Elizabeth's older sister." She tried to steady herself in her high heels. "Indeed."

"Indeed," Ethan echoed her. He motioned to the table. "Have a seat, um—Geraldine."

"Thank you so much," Elizabeth said, gratefully sinking into the chair. "I'm eighteen, by the way."

Ethan rubbed his nose. "Well, pleased to meet you, Geraldine," he said. "Your, um, sister is quite a kid."

"Oh indeed," Elizabeth said, nodding. "She just loves your class. Poetry is practically her life, you know."

"Really?" Ethan leaned forward. "Does she, like, write poetry too?"

"Like?" What kind of word is that for an English teacher to use? Elizabeth oh-so-casually bumped her elbow against Ethan's. "Elizabeth writes OK poetry," she said, "but mine is really quite good, if I say so myself." She gave a discreet cough. "Perhaps you'd like to see it sometime."

It was a good thing she was wearing plenty of rouge, Elizabeth decided. Underneath it all she was positive she was blushing up a storm. No way in the world would the real Elizabeth Wakefield have come on that strong.

Visit the Official Sweet Valley Web Site on the Internet at:

http://www.sweetvalley.com

SWEET VALLEY TWINS
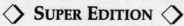 SUPER EDITION

The Twins Go to College

Written by
Jamie Suzanne

Created by
FRANCINE PASCAL

BANTAM BOOKS
NEW YORK·TORONTO·LONDON·SYDNEY·AUCKLAND

SWEET VALLEY TWINS:
THE TWINS GO TO COLLEGE
A BANTAM BOOK : 0 553 50627 7

Originally published in U.S.A. by Bantam Books

First publication in Great Britain

PRINTING HISTORY
Bantam edition published 1998

Conceived by Francine Pascal

Produced by Daniel Weiss Associates, Inc,
33 West 17th Street, New York, NY 10011

Cover photo by Oliver Hunter

Bantam Books are published by Transworld Publishers Ltd,
61–63 Uxbridge Road, London W5 5SA,
in Australia by Transworld Publishers (Australia) Pty Ltd,
15–25 Helles Avenue, Moorebank, NSW 2170,
and in New Zealand by Transworld Publishers (NZ) Ltd,
3 William Pickering Drive, Albany, Auckland.

Printed and bound in Great Britain by
Cox & Wyman Ltd, Reading, Berkshire.

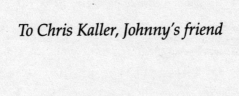

To Chris Kaller, Johnny's friend

One

"A whole summer ahead of us," Lila Fowler remarked happily.

"A whole summer," Jessica Wakefield agreed. The two girls, best friends and sixth-graders at Sweet Valley Middle School, were walking back to Jessica's house after a strenuous trip to the mall. School had just let out a few days earlier, and Jessica was looking forward to a whole summer of mall hopping, sleeping late, sunbathing by the pool, and just generally hanging out.

"Tomorrow we'll go to Chez Foot," Lila said dreamily. "I saw this to-die-for pair of sandals in their window. Gold lamé with silver toe loops. Then maybe we'll hit the beach. The new Belle da Costa swimwear's supposed to be out soon."

Jessica wrinkled her nose. Unlike Lila, who was

the richest girl in Sweet Valley, she couldn't afford to buy the finest of everything. "Or we could go to Casey's and have triple fudge banana splits," she suggested, fingering the coins in her pocket. A triple fudge banana split at Casey's Ice Cream Parlor was definitely worth spending her allowance on. "Or we could just do—nothing at all."

"Nothing at all," Lila echoed. "Let's hear it for nothing at all."

"Hip, hip, hooray," Jessica seconded. *Doing nothing at all was the best part of summer*, she thought. Who needed a schedule, with every minute accounted for, when you could just loll around and do whatever you felt like doing? *When I wake up tomorrow, I might feel like shopping*, she told herself, a smile spreading across her face. *Or I might feel like the beach, or like watching TV, or I might not feel like waking up at all!* "I want to do absolutely everything this summer," she told Lila as they crossed the street. "Except—one thing."

"Which is?" Lila narrowed her eyes.

Jessica tried not to grin too widely. "Go to school!"

"You said it!" Lila agreed.

The two girls turned onto Calico Drive, where Jessica's family lived. Jessica stared up at the blue sky and the fluffy white clouds, feeling the warm sun on her cheeks. "Who needs school anyway?" she asked.

Lila chuckled. "Not me."

"Me neither," Jessica said. "It's not like we don't know half the stuff they teach us. And the other half is pretty stupid. I mean, who needs to know past tenses?"

"And acids and bases," Lila chimed in.

"And what happened in 1842," Jessica went on. She couldn't possibly have cared less what had happened in 1842 unless it had something to do with the invention of sunscreen or building the first shopping mall. But it probably didn't. No, in 1842, Jessica was willing to bet, they were still running around in funny-looking hats trying to shoot turkeys. Any shopping malls would have had turkey stores and funny-looking hat stores, and that would have been it. "And math, yuck, ugh, disgusting."

"You'd think they could have some kind of *decent* curriculum," Lila remarked.

"Yeah." Jessica considered. "Hey! How about shopping mall math!"

"Shopping mall math?" Lila turned to stare.

"Sure." Jessica suddenly felt excited. Why not shopping mall math? "We could, like, compare prices—that's math, right? And count all the swimsuits on sale at Briana Taylor's. And calculate the average weight of a Casey's sundae." *And eat it, afterward of course.* "If we can't get the teachers to go for it, maybe Mom and Dad will, like, homeschool us, and we can just hit the mall every day to do our work." She did her best to look like a serious student.

Lila giggled. "I can see you now, Jessica. 'Hmm, I have to find out which lipstick is the best buy for the money. But first I have to try them all.'" She plastered a prim smirk on her face. "'Excuse me, madame, but this is for a *school project*?'"

Jessica grinned. *A shopping mall curriculum sounded pretty good,* she thought. You could take care of your foreign language requirement by, say, reading the labels on the French perfume bottles and the Italian designer clothes. And you could write reports about which stores had really cool salesclerks and which ones dressed their workers in really dorky uniforms. And as for social studies—

"Jessica!" Lila sounded far away. "You passed your house!"

Oops! Jessica turned quickly—and stepped right into the mail carrier. She'd been so lost in her thoughts, she hadn't even noticed him heading toward her house. Envelopes cascaded to the ground. "Oh no!"

"Head in the clouds again?" Mr. Manetti teased her. He'd been bringing the Wakefields' mail for about as long as Jessica could remember. "Good thing one of us was watching where he was going, or you would have wound up with your head rolling around on the sidewalk!"

Jessica blushed. "I'm really sorry, Mr. Manetti," she apologized. To cover her embarrassment, she bent down to retrieve some of the mail he'd dropped.

"Happens to the best of us." Mr. Manetti grinned. "Here, I think most of that mail is for you people anyway. Why don't you take it up to the house yourself? Save me making a trip." He stared gloomily off into the distance. "When you get old and decrepit, like me, you take advantage of every break you can get."

"Oh no, Mr. Manetti, you're not old and decrepit yet," Jessica wanted to say. But as a piece of mail caught her eye, the words stuck in her throat.

The envelope was addressed to Jessica and Elizabeth Wakefield, and the return address bore the logo of Sweet Valley University, the local college.

"What's wrong?" Lila bent down.

Jessica turned the envelope this way and that, half hoping that the return address would change, but no luck. The red and white SVU initials remained exactly the same. "Oh man," she muttered under her breath.

"Your boyfriend dumping you?" Mr. Manetti teased her.

"SVU?" Lila asked curiously. "You're going to Sweet Valley University already?"

Jessica shook her head. "It's a summer program," she said. Her heart raced. How could she have forgotten the summer program?

A couple of months earlier, Jessica and her twin sister Elizabeth had applied to a summer study program at Sweet Valley University. Elizabeth had been very excited about the program, Jessica re-membered. Studying was exactly the way Elizabeth liked to spend her summers. As for Jessica herself, well, she'd tried very hard not to even apply. Unfortunately, her parents had made her.

"And?" Lila pressed.

Of course, there was always the chance that the letter was a rejection. Jessica didn't exactly believe it. The envelope seemed way too thick. But there was a chance, wasn't there? Jessica licked her lips. No reason to panic—not yet, anyway.

"Come on," she instructed Lila, dragging her friend toward the house.

"Hey, we're in!" Elizabeth grinned and leaned against the kitchen counter, relieved. She read aloud the form letter in her hand one more time, just to be on the safe side. "Dear Jessica and Elizabeth: It is with great pleasure that we notify you that your applications for the SVU summer study program have been accepted." Yes! she thought. She'd been waiting a long time for this let-ter to come.

"Bummer." Jessica pursed her lips. "Are you sure it doesn't, like, say something else? Like, maybe, we accept Elizabeth but not Jessica?"

"Huh?" Elizabeth raised her eyes. Jessica had come barging into the kitchen a moment ago and handed her the envelope with the SVU logo in the corner. "Open it!" she'd commanded, and then she'd plugged her ears and shut her eyes as if afraid the envelope would explode. Elizabeth studied her sister intently. "Don't you want to go?"

"Are you kidding?" Jessica held her nose. "Going to school in the summertime is *exactly* what I had in mind, duh."

Elizabeth sighed. "But this isn't like regular school, Jess," she explained. "It's way better. You take only one class, and you get a long list to choose from. And you get to meet new people. They come from all across the country, practically, for the study program. And we'll stay in the dorms . . ." Her voice trailed off. One look at Jessica's face showed that Jessica wasn't buying it.

"Like I said," Jessica observed dryly.

"Yeah, like she said," Lila chimed in. She made a gagging sound. "Poor Jessica. School in the summertime."

"The only new people I'll be meeting will be nerds and geeks and losers," Jessica said bitingly. "Normal kids stay home in the summer and hang with their *friends*." She scuffed the heel of her shoe on the linoleum. "What's the point of having summer if you can't spend it at the mall and on the beach?"

"I'll be thinking of you," Lila said wistfully, "when I'm lying on the beach in my brand-new Belle da Costa suit, the slinky one with the pink and blue racing stripes—"

"Shut up, Lila." Jessica glared menacingly at her friend.

Elizabeth bit her lip. Jessica could be awfully difficult to deal with sometimes. "It's only for two weeks," she pointed out. "I don't see why you can't put the rest of your life on hold for that long."

Jessica gave a contemptuous snort. "That just shows how much you know."

"Yeah, Elizabeth," Lila said. "You have no idea how complicated your sister's social life is. I mean, if she misses even a few days at the beach . . . "

"Don't remind me," Jessica said, teeth clenched.

"But you'll like it," Elizabeth argued. She opened one of the catalogs that accompanied the acceptance letter. "See, Jess? There are so many really cool courses you could take. Fun with Filmmaking . . . Principles of Engineering: Experiments with Blocks and Rubber Bands . . . Writing Children's Books . . . "

Jessica's only answer was a mournful sigh.

"Well, there *are* interesting courses," Elizabeth said, more to herself than to her sister. Already she had noticed five or six that she was sure she wanted to take, and she hadn't even gotten through the first page.

It's amazing how different we are, she thought. Though the twins looked exactly alike, with long blond hair and blue-green eyes, they were very different people on the inside. While Jessica lived for parties, fashion, and crowds, Elizabeth was happiest curled up on the couch with a good book. Elizabeth spent most of her time hanging out with a few close friends or working on the *Sweet Valley Sixers*, the school newspaper she helped edit. Jessica spent most of her time, on the other hand, gossiping and shopping with Lila and the other girls who made up the exclusive Unicorn Club. And while Elizabeth usually enjoyed her schoolwork, Jessica considered classes a waste of time—at best.

"There's probably a class on acting," Elizabeth ventured, knowing how much her sister liked drama. "Or—" She flipped to the next page, searching for a listing her sister might appreciate. Coordinating fashions, say. Or planning parties.

"Don't waste your breath, Lizzie." Jessica handed Lila a banana and peeled one of her own. "I can tell you without looking, there is absolutely nothing on that whole list that I want to do."

"Do they have shopping mall math?" Lila's eyes were dancing.

"Shopping mall—what?" Elizabeth frowned, puzzled.

"Cut it out, Lila," Jessica snapped. She bit savagely into the banana. "All I want to do is stay home," she said, her words muffled by the sounds of chewing. "Is that so terrible? I mean, is wanting to stay home a crime?"

Elizabeth decided not to say anything. Too bad Jessica didn't like the study program. But it wasn't up to Elizabeth to make her want to go. And Elizabeth was pretty sure that Jessica would like the program if she gave it a chance.

She looked down at the course list again. Scottish Country Dancing . . . Advanced Collage . . . Experiencing Farm Life . . .

How could she ever make a decision?

"I'm not going," Jessica insisted. She waved the acceptance letter from SVU in the air and tried to look even more determined than she felt. This was *serious*. If her parents weren't going to listen to her, she'd wind up at the study program for sure. And if that happened, well, they might as well take her out to the garage and shoot her.

"Of course you are." Mr. Wakefield didn't look up from his newspaper. "It's an honor to be accepted to the study program."

"It certainly is," Mrs. Wakefield agreed. She sat cross-legged on the living room couch, playing solitaire. "Why, when I was your age, I'd have *killed* to get into a study program like the one at SVU."

And I'd kill to stay out of it, Jessica thought, but she decided not to say so. "You mean because you didn't get to, I have to?" she asked ungraciously. Jessica had sulked all the way through dinner, but had waited till she'd done the dishes before making her announcement. "You never got to go mall crawling when you were a kid," she snapped, "so why shouldn't I get to do that, huh?"

Her mother looked amused. "First of all, sweetheart, I did go mall crawling. The Evergreen Plaza was near my house, and my crowd used to hang out there." She laughed. "I can't imagine why. There was a perfectly nice park about a block away."

"Still is," Mr. Wakefield added.

"Evergreen Plaza—yeah, right." Jessica knew she sounded snotty, but she didn't care. "The Evergreen Plaza doesn't count. A crummy movie theater and a grocery store and a bunch of other stores I wouldn't be caught dead in. That's not a *mall*." She made a face, thinking of the garish signs advertising Uncle Frank's Dime Mart—Buy, Buy, Buy! Why wouldn't her parents listen to her? "I mean, it doesn't even have a *roof*."

"Goodness gracious!" Mrs. Wakefield said lightly, playing a red three on a black four. "Not even a roof. I can't imagine what Dyan and Walter and the rest of us were thinking, hanging out in a shopping center that doesn't even have a roof."

Jessica hesitated. Was she being teased? "Anyway, I'm not going," she repeated, folding her arms and staring hard from one parent to the other.

"I think you can take two weeks off from your busy social life," Mr. Wakefield remarked. "Lila and Janet and the others can live without you for a few days. It's not every day that an opportunity like this comes along. Why, you'll meet people from all over the world."

Jessica sighed. How could she explain that she didn't care about meeting anybody *new* right now? That the same old people were perfectly good enough for her, thanks very much? Two weeks without her friends . . . She swallowed hard. By the time she came back, the rest of the Unicorns would have practically forgotten her. "All the friends I could ever want are right here, right now."

Mrs. Wakefield tried to hide a grin. "Well, I wouldn't be too sure about that, honey," she said, shifting a pile of cards to an empty row. "When I went off to college, I met someone who turned out to be very important to me."

Your father, Jessica finished silently. She'd heard this story a million times.

"Your father." Mrs. Wakefield pushed the cards together and leaned back against her husband. "Now what if I'd had your attitude when I went off to school?"

Jessica groaned. "That's, like, completely different, Mom," she said. "You were in college. I'm twelve. You think I'm going to meet the man of my dreams during the next two weeks?" She tried to sound as sarcastic as possible.

"I hope not." Mr. Wakefield put his arm absentmindedly around his wife. "But you will meet interesting people, Jessica, that's for sure."

"Yeah. Nerds and geeks and losers," Jessica muttered.

"Are you calling your sister a nerd, a geek, and a loser?" Mr. Wakefield turned his head inquiringly to Jessica.

"Well—" Jessica considered. Elizabeth could be

a little goody-goody sometimes. And it was hard to deal with her when she did all the research for a report the day it was assigned, while Jessica sometimes waited till the very last minute. Or later. And it was annoying the way Elizabeth always seemed to understand what was going on in math class. Though Jessica had to admit that if she paid as much attention as her sister did, she might do just as well on the tests as Elizabeth. But a nerd? Not exactly. "No," she said after a moment.

"As I thought." Mr. Wakefield turned the newspaper around. A giant headline leaped out at Jessica: Summer Savings at Sweet Valley Mall!!! There was a picture of a model under a beach umbrella, wearing a Belle da Costa swimsuit and holding what looked suspiciously like a Casey's triple fudge banana split. "Jessica, you have to realize that for every nerd and loser who applied to this program, there are at least a dozen regular kids— kids like you and your sister."

"And I'm sure there are interesting courses," Mrs. Wakefield put in.

Jessica set her jaw. "I'm not going," she said again. Her parents just didn't understand. "And you can't make me!"

"Oh but we can," Mr. Wakefield said simply.

"You can't either." Jessica wished she felt as firm as she sounded. "Let Elizabeth go. She's the one who wants to anyway. I'll stay here. I won't even get in your way or anything." She racked her brain to come up with the clincher. "I'll even read three books," she promised.

"Sweetie, you don't understand." Mrs. Wakefield dealt another hand. "Oh good, the ace of diamonds."

"What do you mean, I don't understand?" Jessica demanded. She wished her parents would put their things down and *talk* to her. "If three books isn't enough, I'll read four." *Easy ones,* she added mentally. "I'll even write a report on, um, one of them." She could see herself lolling at the beach, writing away between volleyball matches. "The book was good. I liked it." That kind of thing.

Mrs. Wakefield shook her head. "Didn't we tell you? We're taking the opportunity to go to the Grand Canyon."

"The Grand Canyon?" Jessica curled her lip. *Why would you want to do a thing like that when you could stay here and hang out at the mall?* she wanted to say. Still, the Grand Canyon wasn't so awful. There might be a whirlpool at the hotel, and maybe some hot guys hanging around. For sure, hotter guys than the ones at some stupid summer program at SVU. "Well—OK," she agreed hesitantly. "I'd rather stay here, but the Grand Canyon would be all right, I guess."

Mr. Wakefield shook his head and turned to face his wife. "She really doesn't get it, does she?" he asked.

"Get *what?*" Jessica demanded. She got it, all

right. She was being shipped off to the program against her wishes, and that was kidnapping, wasn't it? Kidnapping or one of those other crimes that people got arrested for. Embezzling, or something. She vaguely remembered seeing someone get put in jail for embezzling on one episode of *Homicide Plus!* "I don't *want* to go to the summer program, OK?" she told her parents. "And if that means that I have to go to the Grand Canyon, then—"

"But you *can't* come to the Grand Canyon with us," Mrs. Wakefield interrupted.

"This is, um, a private trip," Mr. Wakefield explained. He rested his arm on Mrs. Wakefield's shoulder. "It'll be a second honeymoon for us two old fogies."

"Just the two of us," Mrs. Wakefield said. "No kids allowed."

"Anyway," Mr. Wakefield went on with a smirk, "we'll be camping out, and I don't think you'll like that too much."

"No kids?" Jessica had trouble finding her voice. "Camping?" She stared from her mother to her father and back.

Were her parents *crazy* or something?

"So you really don't have a choice, sweetheart." Mr. Wakefield shrugged elaborately. "We can't take you with us, so you'll need to go to SVU."

"But—but—" Jessica's mouth felt dry. Surely there was a way out. "How about—how about I stay home with Steven?" she asked. Steven, her fourteen-year-old brother, was a student at Sweet Valley High. Under normal circumstances, Jessica would rather have died than spend any time at all with her dorky brother, especially alone, but these weren't normal circumstances.

Mrs. Wakefield shook her head. "Steven's going to basketball camp."

"He *is*?" Jessica tried to choke back a feeling of alarm. *This can't be happening!* she thought frantically. "I'll stay home by myself," she burst out. "I'll—I'll do the dishes, and my laundry, and I'll cook . . . " *Most of the time, anyway,* she promised herself. *When I don't go off to Casey's with my friends and have triple fudge banana splits for dinner.* "And I'll pick up my room, every single day, and—and keep an eye on the house—" But even as she spoke, she knew it was no use.

"Jessica." Mrs. Wakefield flashed her a tired smile. "The discussion is over. You're going to SVU—"

"—and you'll like it," her father added. "Really you will."

"And you'll like it," Jessica mimicked under her breath. "Really you will." Glaring at her parents, she stood up with as much dignity as she could muster and walked out of the room, not trusting herself to speak.

I hope you fall into the Grand Canyon! she thought angrily.

Two

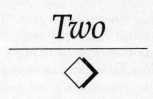

"You poor thing," Mandy Miller muttered. She gave Jessica a brief hug and handed her a black-edged envelope.

It was the day before Jessica and Elizabeth were to leave for their summer study course. The Unicorns were having a slumber party at Jessica's house, and Mandy was the first guest to arrive. Frowning, Jessica slit open the envelope. "With Deepest Sympathy," she read, pulling out the card inside. "Mandy—what is this?"

Mandy didn't crack a smile. "A sympathy card," she explained. "Open it."

A sympathy card? That's what you sent someone when they died, right? Jessica furrowed her brow and flicked the card open. There was a message printed in flowing script on the inside, along with a tasteful picture of pastel-colored roses. "I don't get it," she said, scratching her head.

Mandy nodded solemnly. "Read the message," she suggested. "I heard about your—uh, sad news."

Huh? Jessica stared at her friend. "That's an, um, an interesting outfit," she said, stepping back to see it better. Mandy was dressed in black from head to foot, with a black cape hanging over a black sweatsuit and a little square black hat perched precariously on her head. On anybody else, the clothes might have looked ridiculous, but Mandy had style. "But—why all black?"

"Read the message." Mandy's face was expressionless.

Jessica shrugged and looked down at the card. "At this sad time in your life, know that your friends will always be with you," she read aloud. The card was signed by all the Unicorns—Lila, Mandy, Mary Wallace, Janet Howell, Ellen Riteman, and the rest.

"Well, we won't be *with* you, exactly," Mandy said, "but you'll be in our thoughts, anyway. Hey, guys?" she called behind her.

Jessica blinked. All her friends stood up from behind the shrubbery and came toward the Wakefields' front door. Every one of them was wearing black too.

"We heard you were going off to a summer program," Mandy said, smiling for the first time, "and we thought we'd stop by to extend our deepest sympathy."

"You're so lucky," Elizabeth's friend Amy Sutton said. She sat on Elizabeth's bed and swung her legs over the side.

Elizabeth grinned. Amy was helping her pack for the summer program. "I know it," she said. She couldn't wait to get to SVU tomorrow. "I'm really, really psyched."

"You'll be learning neat stuff," Amy went on, picking up a pile of unmatched socks, "and I'll be going crazy here at home."

"Oh it won't be *that* bad," Elizabeth said. But she felt a twinge of guilt. "I mean, there's the beach, and the mall, and stuff like that."

"The beach and the mall," Amy said dolefully, "which will be taken over with Unicorns. Except your sister, that is."

Elizabeth laughed. She had been invited to join the Unicorns once, but she had turned them down. While she liked some of them individually, she thought they were just a little too shallow when they all got together. Well, OK, a *lot* too shallow. Privately she and Amy called them the "Snob Squad." "You don't *like* hearing Janet Howell and Lila Fowler squealing all over the place?" she asked, feigning surprise.

"In your dreams." Amy rolled two yellow socks together and tossed them into Elizabeth's duffel bag. "You'd better write me every day," she threatened.

Elizabeth smiled. "Every day," she promised. "Unless I have, like, mega-homework."

"What class are you going to take?" Amy wanted to know.

"I don't know yet," Elizabeth admitted. "Not for sure, anyway. There are so many choices." Her copy of the course catalog was on her desk. She'd already marked six or seven classes with stars. "Let's see . . . Cruising the Internet, or maybe What Really Happened to the Titanic? Or there's something about connecting math and art, and then there's always Romantic Poetry."

"Romantic Poetry," Amy echoed, locating two blue socks. She winked at Elizabeth. "Hey, that sounds pretty cool."

Elizabeth felt her cheeks grow hot. "Not *that* kind of romantic," she said defensively. "Romantic with a capital *R*. It's a whole bunch of poets who wrote in a certain style, about specific subjects—nature and people's relationship to it, that sort of thing." *Plus, they wrote about death a lot too,* she reminded herself, but she decided not to say so. "Remember when we read some of them in English class last year?"

"Not really," Amy admitted. "But, you know, Elizabeth, college can be a very romantic place. Without a capital *R*. My parents met when they were at college."

"Did they?" Elizabeth debated whether to take a green T-shirt with the names of all her fifth-grade classmates or a red one with a yogurt company's logo emblazoned across the front. *Better bring the yogurt one,* she decided, folding it neatly. "I didn't know that."

"Yeah." Amy stopped rolling socks and grinned. "Mom's from Sweet Valley, right? And Dad's from Chicago. When they met each other for the first time, it was, like, this little party in some dormitory room. Mom found out that Dad was from Chicago, and she got all snotty and said that L.A. was way nicer. Dad got mad and told her that Chicago was, you know, totally cool, and L.A. was a zoo."

Elizabeth scratched her head. "But if that was how they met, then how—"

"Well, it wasn't exactly love at first sight," Amy admitted. "But then they were in a logic class together the next year, and they used to go around driving all their friends crazy by proving that ham sandwiches are better than eternal happiness. Something like that anyway." She waved her hand carelessly in the air.

Elizabeth raised her eyebrows. "Weird," she said. It seemed like a strange start for a romance.

"And the rest is history!" Amy concluded. She picked up a couple more socks. "So romance is in the air at college," she said meaningfully. "How about you? Where did your parents meet?"

"They met in college too," Elizabeth admitted. "At SVU. But back then it was still called the College of Southern California." She could practically recite the list of all the places that were important to them—the auditorium at the science building where they'd seen movies after dinner; the college bookstore; the coffeehouse that served enormous cookies.

"See?" Amy was triumphant. She put on a fake accent and chanted "Romance is in ze air. *Ro-mance ees een ze air.*"

"Oh stop it," Elizabeth said, feeling a little embarrassed. "It's only for two weeks, and anyway, I'm not going to have time for romance. I'll be too busy with my work."

Amy snickered. "Whatever you say, Elizabeth," she said, "but if you see some cute guy across the lecture hall, promise you'll at least catch his eye." She nudged her friend in the side.

Elizabeth smiled. "I promise," she said.

"We're all so sorry," Ellen Riteman said, extending a black-gloved hand to Jessica.

"Yes indeed," Mary Wallace put in. "And for two whole weeks too! I don't understand how your parents can do this to you."

"Me either," Jessica agreed. She felt very victimized, and she was glad that her friends were rallying around her like this. "They might as well have put me in . . . jail." She led the way down to the rec room. It did feel as if she were going to jail. SVU would probably have armed guards at the doors, pointing rifles at the students and telling them to study, or *else*. And forget anything fun, like going to the beach. She'd be at a college, and what kind of fun did college students have anyway?

Sure, Jessica's parents were always talking about the fun they'd had when they were in college, back in prehistoric times, but all they ever seemed to have *done* was sit around in the dining hall eating apples after lunch. That, and going to movies with subtitles and lots of pictures of people's backs.

And bagpipe concerts. Jessica could imagine nothing worse than going to a bagpipe concert, but her parents had done it several times.

Well, if I'm going off to jail, I might as well enjoy tonight, she consoled herself. Kicking off her shoes, she ran over to the VCR and popped in the first movie she saw.

"What's this one going to be?" Ellen asked curiously. She and Lila gathered around the TV set.

"I'll make the popcorn," Mandy offered.

"I'll set up the sleeping bags," Mary said.

The television screen flickered and suddenly came to life. Pulsating music filled the room, and a cute blond boy a couple of years younger than Jessica pulled up to a fence on a shiny red bicycle. McKinley Carlson, of course—the actor who became famous for screaming. Jessica frowned, trying to remember the name of the movie.

"That's McKinley," Lila said with a note of pride in her voice. "I met him at the film festival in France Daddy took me to last year. Well, I didn't *meet* him exactly, I just almost met him. But we were, like, in the same room together, and I'm almost positive he was looking in my direction once." She sighed. "It was so cool."

"Yeah, right," Janet Howell said dismissively. "I bet you weren't even in the same country as him."

"Was too," Lila shot back. "You're just jealous because you didn't get to almost meet him like me."

"Is he as cute as he looks?" Mary wanted to know.

"Cuter," Lila said breezily.

On the screen, McKinley bent down, smiled his angelic smile, and said something into an intercom. The fence slid apart. McKinley screamed joyously, pedaled hard, and sped through the hole.

Jessica scratched her head. The movie looked familiar. Steven had recorded it some time back, she thought. If she could only remember the name . . .

"I think I've seen this before," Ellen said. "Now he rides off to save the day."

"*After* he gets mixed up with a bunch of bad guys," Mandy added. "And drives them all stark raving nuts."

"No fake." Janet rolled her eyes.

Despite her mood, Jessica burst out laughing. She'd just remembered the name of the movie.

It was called *Jailbreak*.

"I guess I should take these along," Elizabeth said. She pointed to a stack of books that she'd just gotten from the library. "Two of them are Amanda Howard mysteries, new ones that I haven't read yet." Amanda Howard was Elizabeth's favorite mystery writer. The detective in her books was a girl named Christine Davenport. She was brave and smart and kept her head, even when things were at their bleakest. There were times, especially after reading the latest Christine Davenport adventure, that Elizabeth thought she might want to be a detective instead of a writer. "I'm really looking forward to these ones."

"If you take them, you won't write to me," Amy said, the hint of a pout on her face.

Elizabeth laughed. "I'll write to you, Amy, promise." She put the books carefully into the bag. A delicious shiver of anticipation sped through her body. Books 74 and 75 in the series, and Elizabeth just knew they'd be as good as all the rest. Some people said that Amanda Howard didn't really write all the books herself, but Elizabeth knew that wasn't true. Amanda had a writing style all her own.

"She's another one," Amy said.

"Huh?" Elizabeth looked up. "Another what?"

Amy grinned. "I haven't read as many of those books as you have, Elizabeth, but doesn't Christine, like, have a boyfriend?"

Elizabeth wrinkled her nose. "Sure," she admitted. "Ted Thackeray. He's kind of a minor character, though."

"But he's a college student, right?" Amy pressed. "And don't they go to dances and stuff at his campus?"

Elizabeth tapped her chin thoughtfully. Now that Amy mentioned it, it *did* seem like Christine was always going to dances at Eddlestone College, where Ted attended school. *Actually,* she corrected herself, *she's always* planning *to go to dances and things, only the crooks usually waylay Ted's car before they get there, so they work on the case instead.* "Yeah," she agreed slowly. "But—"

"Hey. Like I said." Amy grinned cheerfully and lay back among Elizabeth's pillows. "Ro-mance," she intoned. "Eet ees in ze air!"

"You're silly," Elizabeth said. She reached for a T-shirt and threw it at Amy.

Romance—ha!

"You know, that place doesn't sound so bad after all," Mandy said.

The movie was over. McKinley had screamed fourteen times, by actual count (Mary's), and had been threatened by ten villains. The popcorn had long since been finished. "What place?" Jessica asked.

Mandy snickered. "Don't tell me you've forgotten where you're going tomorrow!"

Jessica squeezed her eyes shut tight. "Thanks for reminding me, Mandy," she groaned sarcastically. "Just when I'd almost forgotten!"

She had, too. She'd been so busy eating popcorn and cheering McKinley on against the crooks, she hadn't had time to think about going off to kid college tomorrow. *Tomorrow* . . . She wished there was some way to put it off.

"Can't you, like, stay with me for the two weeks?" Lila asked wistfully.

"It wouldn't work," Jessica said. She shrugged, feeling totally bummed. "They'd never let me. My parents are always worried about imposing on people."

"Imposing?" Lila stared at Jessica as if she'd said a dirty word. "Jessica, you know you wouldn't be imposing! There are, like, sixty bedrooms in my mansion, and you probably wouldn't even see my dad."

Jessica grinned. Lila's house was the largest in Sweet Valley. It didn't have sixty bedrooms, Jessica was fairly sure, but it did have quite a few. "I—I can't," she said regretfully. "They're going to take me tomorrow and . . . "

"Hey!" Lila brightened. "How about sneaking out after the first day and taking a bus to my house?" Her eyes glittered in the dim light. "Like I said, if you keep out of sight—or if we spend a lot of time hanging at the beach—my dad would never know."

Jessica considered the idea. It was a tempting one. But she shook her head. "No, it'd never work. Elizabeth's going to be there too, and she'd get worried and let people know." *A curse on my sister.*

"But how bad is it, exactly?" Mandy asked. "Have you read the brochure?"

Jessica snorted. "What's the point? I know what it's like." She stroked the back of her neck. "Once we went to my parents' reunion. We got to see the art museum and some classrooms and a nice piece of grassy lawn that we weren't even allowed to run on. Talk about *boring*."

"That's a reunion. That's different." Mandy waved the brochure in the air. "I found this over behind a chair. You ought to read it, Jessica."

"I should?" Something in Mandy's tone made Jessica sit up and take notice. "How come?"

Mandy handed Jessica the brochure. The cover, Jessica saw, had the familiar blue and white SVU logo, along with a picture of some incredibly good-looking students gathering outside a gym. "It says here that SVU's in kind of a funky part of town," Mandy said. "Little coffee shops, delis, stuff like that." She shrugged. "I'm not trying to tell you it's going to be heaven or anything, but maybe it'll be better than you think."

"Yeah, right, Mandy." Janet rolled her eyes.

"Yeah, right," Lila echoed.

Jessica frowned. A hope surged inside her. She opened the brochure. Classrooms . . . bus schedules . . . game room . . .

Game room?

"This place has a *game room*," she said, disbelief

in her voice. Her parents had never said anything about a game room at their college.

"Cool!" Mary whistled.

Jessica stared closely at the picture. The game room looked pretty decent too, with Foosball and Ping-Pong and a whole bunch of Sega machines. "Bruce Patman would go totally crazy in here," she said. Too bad video games weren't exactly her style. But still, if they had video games, they might have other interesting stuff—

"Hey, wow!" Ellen pointed a finger at another paragraph. "'Use of the college pools is free to all students enrolled in the summer study programs.'"

Pools? Heart beating a little faster, Jessica followed Ellen's finger. Quickly she read the text. There were two outdoor pools and an indoor one, plus three Jacuzzis and a sauna. "Hours of Operation," she read in a shaky voice, "7 A.M. to 10 P.M."

Whoa!

"They have wide-screen TVs in each dorm," Kimberly Haver said enviously. "In each dorm! You're so lucky, Jessica."

"And did you see this?" Mary motioned to the back of the brochure. "'Nearby Attractions,'" she read. "'Enclosed Shopping Mall, 3 blocks.'"

Jessica could hardly believe her ears. Quickly, she turned over the brochure. The mall was a big one and even included a tanning salon.

"This is the *dorm* room?" Lila asked, jabbing her

forefinger at a photograph of a room with two large beds.

Jessica stared. She'd imagined a prison cell, practically. But this place looked like a hotel room, only with a bookshelf instead of a TV set. *I could stand a place like that,* she told herself, growing excited.

"Check this out." Mary pointed to a paragraph titled "Policy Statement."

"At Sweet Valley University," Jessica read aloud, her voice quivering with excitement, "we believe that our summer scholars are responsible students able to make choices about their well-being. Though each dormitory floor has its own Resident Advisor, there is no set curfew, no homework check, and no—" She stopped reading. "Yesss!" she sputtered, pumping her fists in the air.

"So you can spend your time at the mall," Kimberly said enviously.

"And in the pool," Mary added. "And at the coffee shops."

"And meeting cute guys like the one in the picture," Mandy went on. "As long as you study a little bit anyway—right?"

Jessica felt a rush of confidence. This was going to be so cool. All she'd have to do was find the easiest course possible, and she'd be absolutely golden. She grabbed her course list from Mandy's grasp and pawed through it quickly. *Advanced Aeronautics . . . no, too hard . . . Cooking for Fun and*

Profit . . . no . . . Weird and Wonderful Americans . . . probably too much reading . . .

Jessica's eyes lit up. *Ceramics.*

Slam-dunk easy *A*! All you had to do was throw some clay together and you had a pot. Big deal. And that would leave the rest of the day free for partying! How hard could it be?

Seizing a red pen, Jessica drew a big jagged circle around the course title.

Now she was thrilled to be going off to SVU!

Elizabeth changed for bed quietly and thoughtfully. Everything was packed, and Amy had left what seemed like hours ago.

Romance? Yeah, right, Elizabeth thought for the fifty millionth time. She flipped idly through the course catalog, to see if something else would stand out and grab her attention. It wasn't like there was any hurry. She didn't have to decide till registration tomorrow, and some of the courses might be closed by the time she got there.

One thing was for sure, she had no romantic plans for the next two weeks. None at all. College was a serious place, even if you were only there for a short while and even if you were only in middle school. It was a place to—what had she told Amy? A place to improve your mind and, um, expand your horizons. Yeah. That was what it was. Not a place to chase boys.

The course listing opened at the class marked Romantic Poetry.

Elizabeth blinked.

On the other hand, romance wasn't exactly the worst thing in the world. If it happened to, like, fall into her lap.

And Romantic poetry could be—well—kind of romantic after all.

All at once she made up her mind. Yanking open her desk drawer, she found a marker and drew a big red circle around Romantic Poetry.

She only hoped there'd still be room when they arrived at SVU tomorrow.

Three

◇

"Oh, the gym," Mrs. Wakefield said with a giggle. She clutched her husband's arm. "Remember that intramural volleyball game when I called for the ball—"

"And I called for it too?" Mr. Wakefield's eyes danced. "And I wouldn't give in, and you wouldn't give in—"

"And we crashed to the floor?" Mrs. Wakefield finished, shaking her head. "You always were a stubborn one, Ned."

"Well, how about you?" Mr. Wakefield shot back. "Talk about stubborn!" He tucked his hand inside his wife's elbow. "But when you got up and glared at me and limped away, you said something I'll always treasure."

A slow grin began to spread across Mrs. Wakefield's face.

"You know what it was, right?" Mr. Wakefield lifted an eyebrow.

"'*When I call for it, buster, I take it!*'" Elizabeth finished in her head. She sighed. How many times had she heard this story? Six hundred? Forty thousand? A million and two?

"'When I call for it, buster, I take it!'" Mr. Wakefield went on, grinning. "And I thought to myself, 'Zing! That's the woman for me!'"

Grown-ups. Elizabeth rolled her eyes. "Um—Dad?" she ventured, pulling gently on her father's sleeve. "Jessica and I have to go find our dorm rooms." She was anxious to meet her new roommate and the other summer study kids who would be living on her floor.

"And register before our classes get filled up," Jessica added. "You guys can do memory lane some other time."

"Really," Elizabeth agreed. She took a quick look back to the family van, piled high with duffels and suitcases. No sooner had the Wakefields arrived at SVU than the twins' parents had begun reminiscing about their college days.

"Then there was the time Walter Egbert and I were playing a little one-on-one basketball," Mr. Wakefield remarked, "and this kid came up and asked to join us. He said he was a freshman, but he looked about ten—"

Elizabeth sighed. She'd heard this story many times too. How the kid had beaten her dad and Mr.

Egbert, even though the kid was about three feet tall, and it turned out that the kid was on the college basketball team and went on to become a star in the NBA. "Come on, Dad," she pleaded. There were butterflies in her stomach. What if she arrived at the dorm so late that everybody already knew everybody else and no one wanted to get to know her?

"Yeah, Dad," Jessica chimed in.

Reluctantly, Mr. Wakefield began walking down through the little business district. "Well, this guy had moves like you wouldn't believe," he was saying. "Walter and I had teamed up against him, and we couldn't have stopped him if we'd had a brick wall! I mean—" *Basketball*. Elizabeth had a sudden idea. "Mom," she broke in, "don't you have to take Steven to his bus today?" Steven was leaving for basketball camp later that afternoon. She checked her watch. "You know, it's *one-fifteen* already," she said, trying to sound as alarmed as possible.

"Oh my! So late!" Jessica opened her eyes very wide. "Shouldn't you leave, like, right now?"

Mrs. Wakefield laughed. "His bus isn't till almost dinnertime. We won't need to leave here for a couple more hours yet."

"Not till three-fifteen," Mr. Wakefield said cheerfully. "So the kid fakes left, dribbles right, and we both fall for it. We're practically in the next time zone by the time the ball falls into the basket!"

Elizabeth groaned.

At this rate, the next two hours were going to be the longest of her life.

"Mo-om," Jessica said loudly. Inside her brain a clock was ticking away. Every minute that went by meant that much less chance to get into the ceramics class.

"Just a minute, sweetie," Mrs. Wakefield replied. Her eyes scanned the menu posted above the counter of the college snack bar. "Oh Ned, look! Chocolate chip milk shakes! We had chocolate chip milk shakes at C.S.C. too, remember?"

"I certainly do!" Mr. Wakefield's voice was hearty. "I didn't think you could find them anywhere else." He stepped up to the counter. "Chocolate chip milk shakes, please," he announced to the waitress. "Four."

Jessica and Elizabeth exchanged panicked glances. Things were getting desperate. "But, Dad!" Jessica said. "I don't want a—"

"Of course you do." Mr. Wakefield clapped her on the shoulder. "This snack bar makes the best chocolate chip milk shakes in the entire world," he said breezily. "Bar none. Many's the time your mother and I would take a study break and come here and drink chocolate chip milk shakes." He patted his stomach. "Of course, I can't do that every day anymore—"

"You never could," Mrs. Wakefield teased him.

"Mom." Jessica clenched her fists. In her mind's

eye she saw the registrar or whoever it was who signed kids up, sitting behind a big old-fashioned desk. She was taking money from some kid and saying, "Oh ceramics? You'll love that one! Lucky you showed up when you did—you just got the last spot!" Jessica swallowed hard. Darned if she was going to take something where she'd have to work—something like The History of the Whole Wide World or A Zillion and One Stupid Science Experiments. "Mom, I don't want a chocolate chip milk shake—"

"Can't we just get set up first?" Elizabeth asked hopefully. "You could stay here and, um, relive old times, and then you could meet us with our stuff later."

"Oh girls." A look of disappointment crossed Mrs. Wakefield's face. "This won't take long. Can't you humor your elderly parents once in a while?"

Jessica stole a quick glance at her watch. Almost two o'clock already. Her stomach churned. "But I really, really want to go sign up for my—"

"Just wait till you taste the milk shakes," Mr. Wakefield promised, licking his lips. "There is nothing quite so good as—"

"Please, Mom," Elizabeth said loudly. "It won't take long, and—"

"Oh Ned!" Mrs. Wakefield gushed. "The honeybuns! Remember how everybody used to buy honeybuns when they had eight o'clock classes and couldn't get to the dining hall for breakfast and—"

Jessica choked back a scream. Angrily, she whirled around to face a candy display. Behind her she could hear the milk shake machine whirring and the excited voices of her parents babbling away. She fingered a box that bore the slogan Candy Is a Nutritious Food. Eat Some Every Day.

No way would there be any spots left in ceramics. No way would there be any spots left in anything remotely good. Not by the time her parents got through going over every single square inch of the entire campus, remembering what had happened on the twelfth of May of their sophomore year and what so-and-so had said at lunch on the first Friday of December when they were juniors.

"It's like liquid candy bar floating down your throat," Mr. Wakefield said.

"Where should we sit?" Mrs. Wakefield asked. "Oh Ned! C.S.C. had a little table by the window just like that one, remember?"

"Where we had that big fight?" Mr. Wakefield finished for her. "How could I forget? Let's go sit there."

Good-bye ceramics, Jessica thought. Ceramics was sure to be one of the most popular courses, now that she thought about it. She was positive that most of the kids who were coming to the study program were only there because their parents made them. And because of the mall and the pool and the other good stuff like that. But like her, they'd be looking for the easiest course of all time.

"Look at these initials . . . remember how everyone carved their initials in the table?" Mrs. Wakefield said, playfully leaning against her husband.

Gag! Jessica gritted her teeth and promised herself that she would never, ever, drag her own kids around her college when she was grown-up.

"This is awful," Elizabeth murmured to Jessica. Two milk shakes had been finished and two others left on the table, and the girls were now striding across the campus in search of the auditorium to see if it was anything like the one where their parents had performed with the college choral society.

"You said it." Jessica shook her head tiredly. "Why won't they just go and leave us alone?"

"They said they wanted to relive old times," Elizabeth said sadly. "But you and I will be old ourselves by the time they're finished."

"The music building!" Their father's voice boomed back to the twins. "Hey, kids, the music building was where your mother and I heard that crazy poet read from his work!"

"Like, wow," Jessica hissed to Elizabeth. "Pardon me while I faint."

"Yeah, and it was so awful we left after ten minutes," Mrs. Wakefield remarked.

Elizabeth didn't think she could stand to hear yet *another* chapter from the life of her parents. "Mom—," she began. It was time to let them know exactly how she felt.

"And look, Ned, the clock tower on the edge of the quad," Mrs. Wakefield was saying. "What was that slogan carved into it? Climb high, soar free—"

"You want an *A*, but get a *D*," Mr. Wakefield finished with a laugh. "That's how I remember it, anyway."

Clock tower. Elizabeth fought off the feeling of time closing in around her. If she didn't get into the dorm soon, she'd—she'd—well, whatever she would do, her parents wouldn't like it, that was for sure.

"Now, Ned," Mrs. Wakefield said reprovingly. "It was something else—something inspiring. Take a look, kids."

Unwillingly Elizabeth lifted her eyes to the tower—and froze.

The huge iron hands of the clock were pointing to precisely 3:15.

3:15! How could it be 3:15 already? "That can't be right," she muttered, rolling up her sleeve and looking at her watch. Just as she had thought, two-fifteen. She breathed a little more easily. There was still time. The clock was just an hour fast, that was all. Or it was stopped. Maybe when—

Wait a minute.

"So you like the old tower, huh?" Mr. Wakefield rumpled Elizabeth's hair.

Elizabeth drew in her breath and tried to look alarmed. "Look at the clock!" She jabbed a forefinger at the tower. "*What* time did you say you had to leave?" *And don't look at your watches!* she commanded them in her mind, hoping that ESP worked.

"Oh man!" Mr. Wakefield thwacked himself on the forehead. "Time sure flies when you're having fun! OK, back to the car, girls. I hope you don't mind if we drop you off and get going—do you?"

Elizabeth winked at Jessica. It was the easiest question she'd ever had to answer.

"No problem!" the twins said at the exact same instant.

Four

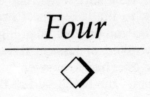

"Woodbridge Hall," Jessica said thoughtfully, looking down the hallway of their dormitory. "Wonder who Mr. Woodbridge was."

Elizabeth smiled. "Might have been Ms. Woodbridge, you know," she pointed out. "Either way, I bet they gave lots and lots of money to SVU."

Jessica grinned back. She was nervous but happy. The girls had dropped their stuff off in their rooms, which were on the same floor, and rushed off to sign up for their courses. Jessica had been lucky—ceramics hadn't been closed. And Elizabeth had gotten into her first choice too: Romantic Playwriting or Redundant Poetry or some such thing, Jessica wasn't sure.

"Think our roommates will be there yet?" Elizabeth asked.

Jessica shrugged. Their rooms had been empty when they'd gone in. "I hope so," she said. She was looking forward to meeting her new roommate. The girl was named Susan, Susan Rainer, according to a long list that the Resident Advisor had posted at the front entryway.

"Me too." Elizabeth pushed a strand of hair out of her eyes. "Marion Hobart's my roommate. I wonder what she'll be like."

Probably kind of a dork, Jessica thought, but she didn't say so aloud. "Marion Hobart" sounded like a kid who would be pretty serious about school, she decided. She pictured Marion with big thick glasses and short-short hair. Maybe a little overweight. Marion would be nice enough, she thought, but she'd be hopeless when it came to doing anything cool. Not exactly Unicorn material. Elizabeth was welcome to her.

Now, Susan . . . well, Susan, on the other hand, would be cool. Maybe even awesomely cool. Marion might come from some dinky town in the middle of the desert or something, but somebody named Susan Rainer would definitely come from L.A. or Seattle, someplace big and exciting. She'd listen to the right music, wear the right clothes. *Yeah.* Jessica grinned to herself. She and Susan would get along fine.

"Hello?" Elizabeth paused outside her door.

"Hi!" A friendly voice floated out into the hall. "You're Elizabeth, right? I'm Marion. Come on in!"

Curious to see how well her mental picture of Marion fit, Jessica tagged along after her twin. To her surprise, she saw a girl who looked very much like herself standing by a bookshelf, unpacking.

"Whoa! I'm seeing double!" Marion waved her hand frantically before her eyes.

Elizabeth laughed. "Twins, that's all. This is my sister, Jessica."

Standing up, Marion extended a hand. "Nice to know you, Jessica. So here's my question—are you guys twins, or are we triplets?"

Elizabeth caught her breath. "We do look a lot alike," she said doubtfully. She stretched out her arm and pointed first to Marion, then to Jessica. "See, Jess? Blond hair, blond hair. The same length too. Blue-green eyes, blue-green eyes." She bit her lip. "We're the same height. And—and her expression's the same as mine."

Triplets? Jessica stared at Marion's eyes. The girl had a look on her face that—that looked like Elizabeth. Jessica's heart gave a leap. "You aren't serious, are you?" she ventured. A wild thought rose in her. *Maybe there were three of us, really, and Mom and Dad couldn't afford to keep us all, so they let Marion go and be adopted by some other family, and . . .*

"Nah." All at once Marion seemed to shrink a couple of inches. She smiled broadly, and Jessica exhaled. Marion's expression no longer looked anything like Elizabeth's. "We look alike on the surface, is all."

"But—weren't you just taller?" Jessica asked. It sounded like a stupid question, but she couldn't think of another way to ask it.

Marion laughed. "Not exactly. I made you *think* I was taller. You can do that, you know, if you practice a lot. I got the idea from this book." She thumped a volume on the bookshelf in front of her. Jessica frowned at it. The book was called *Master of Disguise*, and it had a drawing of a false mustache on the front. "And as for putting on other people's expressions, well, I've learned to do that too."

"You have?" Elizabeth sounded unbelieving.

"I sure have." For a brief instant Jessica saw her own face flash across Marion's features. The effect was astonishing. It was just like looking into a mirror. Then Marion's face reappeared. "See?" she said, sounding pleased with herself.

"I—I see," Jessica stammered.

"That's so cool," Elizabeth remarked. "Would you mind if I, like, looked through your book sometime over the next couple of weeks?"

Marion gave a shrug—a shrug, Jessica noticed, that looked a little like her sister's shrugs. "Be my guest."

"You can be our honorary third twin," Elizabeth suggested. "Now that you're not trying to look like us, I can see a bunch of differences. Can't you, Jess?"

"Oh yeah," Jessica agreed. It was disconcerting to meet someone who could make herself look like you at will, and she was glad to see differences. "Like, she is shorter. That's obvious when you look."

"And her face is thinner, I think," Elizabeth added.

"And her eyes are a little bit more blue," Jessica went on. "And her hair doesn't have waves like ours." She smiled. It was silly how she'd thought at first that Marion might actually be a long-lost triplet. Now that she looked closely, she could tell that they looked way different.

All the same, she thought uneasily, she had been very wrong about what Marion looked like. Overweight, glasses, short hair—wrong, all wrong.

"I'll catch you two later," she said, waving to Marion and Elizabeth. "I'm going to see if my roommate's around yet."

And to see if I was as wrong about her as I was about Marion! she thought, walking briskly out of the room and down the hall.

"You must be . . . Jessica."

The girl on the bed put down the latest issue of *More Beautiful You Monthly* and surveyed Jessica, her eyes flickering from Jessica's shoes to her head and back. She yawned and shuddered slightly. "Oh dear."

"Oh dear?" Jessica repeated blankly. Susan Rainer—at least, she assumed that this girl was Susan—was beautiful, all right. She had long silky dark hair and near-perfect skin. "What do you mean—'oh dear'?"

Susan's lip curled slightly. "Nothing," she said, and her face broke into a bright smile. "Just your clothes—well, never mind that. I'm Susan, Susan Rainer if you hadn't guessed." She picked up her magazine again, the smile disappearing as quickly as it had come. "I get the bed away from the window, by the way," she said languidly. "The early morning sunshine does terrible things to my skin. Not that it would affect *yours*."

Jessica frowned. Her clothes? What exactly was wrong with her clothes? She stared down at her T-shirt and jeans, wondering if maybe she should have worn a skirt like the one Susan had on. And what was this about the early morning sunshine? "Um—I'm, like, pleased to meet you," she said in the friendliest voice she could muster.

"Like, so am I." Susan yawned and flipped to the next page.

Jessica licked her lips. Somehow she'd sensed a . . . a hint of meanness in Susan's tone of voice. What was that vocabulary word she'd had in school that meant, like, putting somebody down by thinking you were better than they were? Pat . . . pate . . . patronizing, that was it. She narrowed her eyes, wondering if Susan was being patronizing to her. "I'm sure we have a lot in common," she said.

"Yes, tons." Susan's eyes didn't leave her magazine. "I know high fashion. You wear T-shirts." She smirked. "I'm from L.A. You're from the middle of the desert."

The middle of the desert? "What are you talking about?" Jessica demanded hotly. "I live right here in Sweet Valley!"

"Oh *please*." Susan yawned again and stretched. "Like Sweet Valley isn't in the middle of the desert. The cultural desert, anyway. Where can you go to see a good French film with subtitles, or buy the latest Syrian bread? Have you ever eaten Syrian bread?" She flashed Jessica a cat-that-ate-the-canary grin. "I didn't think so."

Jessica swallowed hard. Obviously Susan thought she was a nobody. "I've been to L.A. lots of times," she said breezily. "I've been to clubs and everything. My dad took me to a jazz concert once even." She hadn't liked it very much, but Susan didn't need to know that, and maybe a jazz concert would impress Susan.

"Your *dad*." Susan smiled in a way that Jessica was sure was patronizing. "It's funny. Kids from the suburbs are so—so fixated on their parents, while kids from the city are so—" She gave a toss of her shoulders. "So independent."

Jessica took a deep breath. This wasn't going well at all. "If you think Sweet Valley is so boring, what are you doing here?"

Susan laughed lightly. "I'm sure *you're* here for the classes," she said, drawing out the last word as if it had rabies. "Typical nerd, yes? I'm here FTB."

"FTB?" Jessica hated to admit that she wasn't up on the latest slang, but she didn't see any way out. "What's—FTB?"

Susan's eyes gleamed. "*For the boys.* Of course."

"I see." Jessica grinned. For the boys. "I can, um, relate." At last, a connection between her and her new roommate.

A humorless giggle escaped Susan's mouth. She rolled over on the bed and faced the wall. "You?" she said over her shoulder. "Wearing the clothes that *you've* got on right now?"

There was a pause.

"I don't think so," Susan said in a crushing voice.

"Romantic Poetry?" Marion leaned against the dresser and studied Elizabeth with interest. "Cool! I've always, you know, admired people who can do poetry."

"Oh I wouldn't say I can do poetry, exactly." Elizabeth felt a little embarrassed. "It's just—well, it's fun. Words are so neat. What are you taking?"

Marion waved a casual hand in the air. "Criminology," she said.

"Criminology?" Elizabeth was impressed. "You mean, like, the study of criminals?"

"Close enough." Marion grinned. "It's sort of what makes criminals tick. It's also ways of catching crooks. Fingerprints, tracing phone calls, things like that. Both my parents are police detectives, and

I want to be one too." She looked down at her feet. "Not to brag or anything, but I can pick the locks on handcuffs already. Most of the time, anyway."

"Really?" Elizabeth raised her eyebrows. Her mind was whirring. "You want to be a detective, huh? What do you have to do to be a good detective—besides take classes in criminology, I mean?"

"You have to be a good observer," Marion said slowly. "It helps to be a master of disguises, like I'm studying how to do, and it helps to learn to, you know, *think* like a criminal. But observation is number one." She clapped her hand suddenly across her chest and whirled around. "Let's do a test. Bet you can't tell me what my T-shirt says."

Elizabeth frowned. Of course she knew the answer to that question. She'd been staring at Marion's T-shirt for the last fifteen minutes, right? "Um—," she began. "It's, it's white, and—"

"You can tell that from the back," Marion pointed out.

"True." Elizabeth couldn't help but smile. She closed her eyes, the better to think clearly. *There's a picture of a bear or something,* she told herself, *and black letters. And the first word begins with a* D—*no, a* G. "Um—," she said, stalling for time.

Marion laughed. "You don't remember, do you?"

"No," Elizabeth admitted sheepishly. "Turn around and let me see."

"Ta-dah!" Marion spun back to face Elizabeth,

who opened her eyes and gulped. The shirt was completely blank. "See?" Marion said. "It's all in the observation. But you can learn that too," she added helpfully. "Anyone can. There's no trick; you just have to *look*."

"Do you read mysteries?" Elizabeth asked. She held out her new Amanda Howard books for Marion to see. "This is my all-time favorite series."

"Amanda Howard? Oh sure," Marion said carelessly. "I used to read them a lot when I was younger. But they're not as satisfying now." She sighed. "I mean, the adventures are fun and everything, but, really, Christine Davenport could stand to take a few criminology classes. Some of the police methods she applies are so old-fashioned. . . ." Her voice trailed off.

"Yeah?" Elizabeth twisted a lock of hair. She'd never thought of Christine as being out of date. "Um—like what?"

"Well." Marion chuckled. "Like in book 37, when she picked up the suspect's wallet in her bare hands?" She whistled softly. "That's a *huge* no-no. You could get your own prints all over the leather and zowie, there goes your chain of evidence. Or in book 67, when she's following that guy around town and doesn't wear a disguise even though they'd just talked in the chapter before." Marion laughed hollowly. "Like, I'm *sure* my parents would always get their man if they tailed people like that."

"I see." Elizabeth swallowed hard and set the books down on a chair. "Well, are there authors who *are* up-to-date on their police methods?"

"You bet," Marion said. "But tell you what. Why don't we talk about that in the snack bar?" Her eyes danced. "I'm thirsty, and I'd like to see a little more of the campus anyway."

"Sure!" Elizabeth was ready for a snack herself. "OK if we stop by Jessica's room and invite her and her roommate too?"

"No problem." Marion grabbed her disguises book. "I'll bring this along, if you don't mind. I study every chance I get. Have you been to the snack bar yet?"

Elizabeth smiled. "Not exactly," she said. "But I hear they make a really tasty chocolate chip milk shake."

"You have *got* to help me," Jessica hissed across the snack bar table at her sister. Her stomach churned. Next to her Marion leafed idly through the pages of her disguises book. Jessica angrily jabbed her straw into her own cup. "Susan is an absolute first-class grade *A* snob, is what she is."

Elizabeth twisted her napkin. "I'm sorry you don't like her, but what do you want me to do?" she asked.

Jessica gritted her teeth. She hated it when Elizabeth got all reasonable like this. First the twins had been really nice and kind and everything and invited Susan to come along to the snack bar with them, and Susan had tossed her head in that annoying way she had and said, "Well, I guess there's nothing better to do," and she'd been sitting there ever since yawning and talking about her horoscope until she'd suddenly gotten up in the middle of one of Jessica's stories and walked off to the bathroom, and—and if this was the way Susan was going to treat her, then Susan could just go fry, that was what she could do. Jessica widened her eyes at Elizabeth. "I don't care what you do," she snapped. "Just do *something!*"

Elizabeth shook her head. "If you really don't like it, you can go to the main office or something and put in for a change."

"That would be tomorrow," Jessica protested. "I can't wait that long." A sudden thought struck her. "Hey! Tell you what. Let's have you and me switch rooms, OK? I'll room with Marion, and you can room with . . . with her."

"Yeah, right," Marion said without looking up.

Elizabeth laughed. "You don't really expect me to jump at that offer, do you? If you don't like her, how do you expect me to like her any better than you?"

"Because—" Jessica considered. "Because you always see the good side in everybody."

"I'm sure Susan must have one," Elizabeth said gently.

"I doubt it," Jessica said gloomily.

Marion looked up. "I doubt it too. The way she's been talking so far—wow." She shook her head. "And don't go thinking that the two of you could room together and I'd move in with the Ice Queen. Over my dead body." She made a slashing motion across her throat and returned to her book.

Jessica raised her eyebrows. How had Marion guessed exactly what she'd been thinking?

"Live with it," Elizabeth suggested. "If you're lucky, she won't be around much. Anyway, there are tons of other kids here. You'll meet lots of nice people."

Jessica nodded slowly. She'd seen signs for a dozen groups around the campus. The Nature Scouts' Convention . . . the Boys' Chorale Competition. There was a cheerleading camp, a baseball camp, and a drama workshop. Debate training. A student government group. Some of the kids would no doubt be dweebs and losers, but the rest . . . She nodded slowly.

"Hi. I'm Mike. Mind if I sit down?"

The voice was almost at her elbow. Jessica turned and found herself staring into a pair of the softest brown eyes she'd seen in a long time. "Sure," she said, moving over to let Mike sit down.

"Gee, thanks!" Mike flashed her a quick smile. "What are you here for?" he asked, plunking a glass of orange pop down on the table. "I'm from Oregon, and I'm a Nature Scout. We're going canoeing in a few days, but till then we'll be around."

Jessica couldn't help staring. Mike was very handsome, she decided. "Um—I'm here with the summer study program," she said, tossing her head the way she'd seen Susan do it. "I'm studying ceramics."

"Ceramics?" Mike grinned. "Cool!"

"I don't believe I know you." Jessica jumped. Susan was back. Ignoring Jessica, she sat down and leaned close to Mike. "I'm Susan. Susan Rainer that is. You are—"

Mike swallowed hard. "Mike." He turned to face her.

"So, um, where in Oregon are you from?" Jessica ventured, hoping to get Mike to look back in her direction.

"I'm from L.A.," Susan said in a world-weary voice, batting her eyelashes.

"Oh, L.A.!" Mike brightened. "I've always wanted to live in L.A. That must be, like, so totally awesome."

"It gets to be a bit of a bore now and then," Susan said, smiling directly at Mike. "But mostly it's very satisfactory. Do you like jazz?"

"L.A. isn't actually all that different from Sweet Valley," Jessica broke in. She didn't like the way Mike was looking at Susan. "Which is where I live."

"Oh, the suburbs," Susan said languidly.

"I'd just think—I mean, there are so many *people* in L.A.," Mike went on. "That would be so neat, to have all that stuff going on—"

"Lots of stuff happens in Sweet Valley too," Jessica argued.

Susan adjusted her shoulder so it was practically in Jessica's face. "Well, there are certainly some wonderful things about the big city," she purred. "Like you wouldn't see outfits like hers every day of the week." She glared, steely-eyed, at Jessica and muttered something that sounded like "Thank goodness."

Jessica clenched her fists. "So what's wrong with my outfit?" she demanded. Bad enough that Susan was talking to Mike, but to have her throw insults at the same time. . . . "I happen to *like* T-shirts and jeans."

Susan trilled a little laugh. "Some people just don't get it," she said. "Come on. Let's find a private table where you and I can be together."

Jessica watched, speechless, as Susan stood and helped Mike to his feet. Without glancing back once, Mike seized his soda and followed Susan into the crowd milling around the snack bar.

"Amazing," Marion said with a snort. "What a jerk."

"I—I can't believe she did this to me." Jessica shook her head, tight-lipped. She had never felt so completely put down in her entire life.

Elizabeth toyed uneasily with her straw. "Come on, guys, don't be so harsh. She must have some nice qualities."

"Not Susan Rainer," Marion said cheerfully.

"You can say that again," Jessica grumbled.

If Susan Rainer had a good side, she'd trade in all her Johnny Buck albums . . . and buy jazz instead!

Five

It's amazing how interesting the campus is when there aren't parents around to clutter it up, Elizabeth thought.

After dinner, she'd gone out for a walk by herself to explore. She'd hit the library, the soccer field, and the foreign language building with its big *Bienvenue!* banner out front. Now it was getting dark, and she was heading back to her dorm room. "College is cool," she murmured. A slow smile spread across her face. "College is *definitely* cool." She couldn't wait for her poetry class to begin tomorrow. . . .

A few kids rushed across a nearby footbridge, laughing and talking. Elizabeth glanced up at the clock tower, wondering what time it was. Then she laughed. The hands of the clock were still stuck at

3:15. "Thanks, clock," she said aloud, saluting it smartly.

A line of poetry ran through her head as she climbed up the bridge. Something about clocks striking while someone was on a bridge . . . "'I stood on the bridge at midnight,'" she said softly, pausing and looking across the grassy quad, "'when the clock was striking the hour.'" *No, that's not quite right.* "'The *clocks*,'" she corrected herself. "'When the clocks were striking the hour.'"

There was silence. And suddenly Elizabeth was struck by a thought. Why not yell out the line, as if she were in a play or something? She knew it was a very un-Elizabeth-like thing to do, but then again, this was college. No one was around. No one she knew anyway. College was a time to take on new identities, wasn't it?

She looked back and forth and bit her lip. Did she dare?

Sure—why not!

Elizabeth stood on tiptoe, stretched out her arms imploringly toward the tower clock, and spoke in her most dramatic voice. "'I stood on the bridge at midnight,'" she called, "'when the clocks were striking the hour'" She held still, listening to the sound bounce back toward her off the buildings. *There,* she thought happily. *That felt—*

"Longfellow," said a voice behind her.

Heart beating furiously, Elizabeth whirled around.

If she'd known anyone had been listening . . . "W-What did you say?" she stammered.

A boy was standing there in the darkness, a boy with light hair and an engaging, slightly toothy smile. "Longfellow," he said pleasantly. "The poem you were quoting just now. It's by Henry Wadsworth Longfellow, isn't it?"

Elizabeth took a deep breath. She was embarrassed at having been overheard. "Longfellow, that's right," she said. "It's called—"

"'The Bridge,'" the boy supplied helpfully. "I thought so. It's one of, um, my personal favorites."

"Oh!" Elizabeth blinked. She hadn't thought there would be many boys on campus who knew about poetry. "Do you like—" She found herself turning faintly pink. "Do you like poems a lot?"

The boy took a step backward. "Um—you could say that," he said shyly, running a hand through his hair.

"Really?" Elizabeth stepped forward excitedly. "Do you have a favorite poet?" Then, worried that she was coming on too strong, she smiled and leaned against the rail of the bridge. "Not that you *have* to have one or anything. It's just that—"

The boy smiled, and his grayish eyes twinkled in the harsh glare of the streetlights. "Oh, I like Longfellow a lot," he said. "'Hiawatha' and 'Paul Revere.' And 'The Wreck of the Hesperus.'"

"And 'Under the spreading chestnut tree'?" Elizabeth asked. She'd always liked that poem, about a village blacksmith with muscles "strong as iron bands."

"That too." The boy nodded. "Do you know 'The Arrow and the Song'? 'I shot an arrow into the air,'" he quoted, and looked expectantly at Elizabeth.

"'It fell to earth, I knew not where,'" Elizabeth said, nodding slowly.

"And the third stanza?" The boy smiled his toothy smile. "That's, like, the best of all, I think. 'And the song, from beginning to end,'" he recited slowly, "'I found in the heart of a friend.'"

"That's—nice." Elizabeth swallowed hard. "I didn't, um, know that part."

"No?" The boy looked like he might be about to say something else, but then he looked down at the ground and gave a shrug. "Well. Good to meet you. I guess I'll see you around," he mumbled, and disappeared down the sidewalk.

The heart of a friend. Elizabeth watched him go, half wanting to call him back so she could at least ask his name.

She hoped she *would* see him around.

After all, it wasn't every day that you met a guy who was interested in poetry!

"You know," Jessica said, measuring her words carefully, "I didn't like what you did. Back in the snack bar, I mean." She rested her arms on her hips and stood facing Susan, who was lying on her bed.

Next to the bed, sounds of a jazz combo drifted out of Susan's tape recorder.

Susan's eyes flicked momentarily to Jessica's face and then back to the fashion magazine in her hand. "Imagine that," she said sarcastically. "I wasn't, like, trying to please *you* or anything, you know."

"Yeah, I kind of guessed that," Jessica said. She took a deep breath, trying to stay calm. Susan was pushing all her buttons. "And I didn't like what you said about my clothes either."

"Your clothes?" Susan repeated, sitting straight up. "How could I *not* say anything about your clothes? I mean, is this how they *teach* you to dress here in the suburbs?"

Jessica crossed the room and savagely pressed the Off button on the cassette player. A solo trumpet cut off in midscreech. "Listen to me," she insisted through gritted teeth.

"Listen to you?" Susan gave a brittle laugh and stood up from the bed. "Why would I want to do a juvenile thing like *that?*" She hit the Play button on the tape recorder. The trumpeter resumed playing as if nothing had happened. "You don't *appreciate* jazz, do you?" She folded her arms and smirked at Jessica. "What do you listen to here in the sticks?"

Jessica laughed hollowly, but inside she was seething. "I happen to like *real* music. Johnny Buck and those guys."

Susan raised an eyebrow. "Pop music," she went

on in a bored voice. "I might have known. Talk about clueless. Come to the city sometime, *kid*, and I'll show you what *real* music is like."

Kid. Jessica clenched her fists. Who did Susan think she was calling a kid? She would gladly have hit Susan right in the middle of her obnoxiously perfect face. "Me a kid? You're the one who's so immature," she remarked, blinking her eyes furiously. "How old are you anyway?"

"Twelve." Susan sighed in that obnoxious way she had, making it seem as if Jessica was about two.

If Jessica ever had "patronizing" as a vocabulary word again, she'd just summon up a picture of Susan Rainer, and *poof!* "Yeah, but when's your birthday?" she demanded. She'd show Susan who was older.

Susan flashed Jessica a killer smile. "I'm not talking *chronological* maturity," she said, settling herself back on the bed. "I'm talking *emotional* maturity. And it's obvious that I'm, like, eighteen and you're six."

Sparks flashed in front of Jessica's eyes. Nobody, but nobody, said things like that to Jessica Wakefield and got away with it. "Yeah?" she sneered. She hated Susan. Hated, hated, hated, hated. "Well, guess what I'm going to do. I'm going to go to the Resident Advisor and get your room changed. That's what I'm going to do." *Any* roommate would be better than this—this snot masquerading as a girl.

Susan laughed. "Why don't you do that," she said. "But before you leave, I have a present for you."

Jessica paused on her way to the door. "What?" she asked suspiciously.

Susan tossed her copy of *Young Urban Sophisticate* to her. "Read it, *kid*," she said contemptuously. "Who knows, you might even learn something!"

"He was soooo cute," Elizabeth said dreamily. She lay on her bed, a grin plastered across her face. "But he wouldn't even tell me his name."

"Wouldn't, or didn't?" Marion asked. She was at her desk, leafing through her disguises book.

"Didn't, I guess." Actually, Elizabeth decided, the whole thing had been right out of a Romantic poem. In Romantic poetry, truly cute guys were always meeting up with beautiful girls. *Well, semi-beautiful girls,* she corrected herself, fingering her hair. And lots of times, the guys were running away or dying or something like that, so they were in disguise and they didn't want to tell the girl who they really were. And then the two of them would never see each other again, and the girl would spend, like, the rest of her life pining away for the guy, and it was all noble and exciting and brave and—well, romantic.

Marion flashed her a knowing look. "If you want, I could make some inquiries," she said.

"That's what detectives do when they go around asking about a crook." She sketched a head in the air. "See, you could draw a sketch of what he looks like, and then I could take it all over campus, asking who knows him. Only I'd be, like, discreet, so nobody would know why I wanted him."

Elizabeth scratched her head. It was an interesting idea. "Well—"

"Of course, you'd have to be willing to pay," Marion interrupted. "People don't give away what they know. You'd need tens and twenties to get what you wanted out of your informants."

Elizabeth's jaw dropped. "Tens and—twenties?" she gasped.

Marion shrugged. "It's the way a real police force operates. You don't have to like it, but you do have to live with it."

Tens and twenties. Elizabeth's mind reeled. "But—but Christine Davenport never, ever pays for information," she ventured.

Marion rolled her eyes. "Like I said, Amanda Howard doesn't know about the most up-to-date police methods." She sat forward and grinned. "Or, if you want, I could follow him," she said, her face gleaming with excitement. "I'm getting pretty decent at that."

"Follow him?" Elizabeth felt that she was getting out of her depth. "But if I don't know who he is, how can you—"

"Elizabeth!" The door flew open. Jessica stood in

the hall, a furious expression on her face. "I need to talk to you this minute!"

Thoughts of the cute guy faded from Elizabeth's mind. "What's the problem?"

"It's my so-called roommate," Jessica said through clenched teeth. "Susan the Aardvark. If I don't get rid of her, my life is ruined."

"Ruined?" Elizabeth couldn't help grinning. *Drama in real life*, she thought. "So what's the scoop?"

"She's just so—ugh," Jessica said with feeling. "She's like a spider, only worse. She said the most unbelievably awful things to me, Elizabeth, you can't even imagine."

"What?" Marion piped up. "I bet it wasn't as bad as what the bank robber called my mom after she snapped the bracelets on him—"

"Worse," Jessica barked. "And so I went to the RA, and told her that I'd probably jump off a bridge if she didn't find Susan a new room double-quick, and you know what she said?"

Elizabeth thought she probably could guess.

"She said there were no rooms left!" Jessica plopped down on Marion's bed. "And I said I'd take, like, a closet, and she said they'd given the closets out too."

"So you're stuck," Marion said cheerfully.

"And *then* she had the nerve to say that maybe because we were so different, we'd learn something from each other," Jessica went on, making a face. "The woman is hopeless. Like I could possibly learn anything from—" She leaned forward and her eyes took on a sudden gleam. "But, see, I had this idea."

"Uh-oh." Elizabeth groaned. "This is what it's like to be Jessica's twin, Marion. She always has some wild idea or other."

"Never a dull moment," Marion observed.

"Well, I wouldn't call this one a wild idea, exactly," Jessica protested. "It's just that—well—Elizabeth, change rooms with me already!"

"Oh, Jessica." Hadn't they already been through all that at the snack bar? Elizabeth sighed. "I'm not going to switch, and that's final."

"If you want I'll run some background checks on her," Marion offered. "I bet she isn't what she's cracked up to be," she added darkly. "After all, we only have her word for it that she even comes from L.A."

Elizabeth frowned. It was true. College was a place where you could, like, take on new identities. She'd sort of learned that this evening. What if Susan was just acting a part?

"Elizabeth?" Jessica was on her knees now. "Be a pal. Please?"

Elizabeth hated saying no to her sister, but she wasn't about to let Jessica push her around. Not here at college.

"Deal with it," she said.

And she felt only a little tiny bit guilty too.

Six

◇

Promptly at nine on Monday morning, Jessica walked into her ceramics room and tossed a backpack on the table. She was psyched to get away from Susan, even if that meant going to class. Fortunately, it was a slam-dunk easy *A* class. Three hours or so of this and she'd be on her own. Free to hit the mall, the pool, the Jacuzzi . . .

"Ladies and gentlemen." The teacher, a small, stoop-shouldered old man with a trace of a foreign accent, rapped a ruler for attention. "Welcome to ceramics."

"Thank you," Jessica murmured, taking a seat on one of the high stools that surrounded the tables. She stole a quick look at her classmates. There were lots of guys. Lots of really good-looking guys. One boy in the corner reminded her a little of Bruce

Patman, the most gorgeous kid at SVMS. And another guy had a serious expression but a hint of mischief in his brown eyes . . .

Weird, she thought. She wouldn't have expected so many macho guys in a course like ceramics. Not that she was complaining or anything. In fact . . .

Her eyes roved around the room. There were, like, three guys to every girl. And was it her imagination, or were several of the guys . . . *looking* at her? She was almost sure they were.

"I am sure you will enjoy the working with clay," the teacher was saying. He fingered his mustache and sat down at the enormous potter's wheel in the front of the room. "You will find there is nothing quite as *relaxing* as putting your hands in a soft piece of clay and producing an exquisite object of art."

Jessica felt eyes on the back of her neck. She shifted slightly on her stool.

"I predict that this class will give you the best memories of your young lives," the teacher went on.

Jessica smiled.

With all the guys in the class, she had a feeling her teacher would be absolutely right!

"Where's the prof anyway?" the girl next to Elizabeth asked.

Elizabeth frowned and checked her watch. Five after nine already. The small lecture room where the poetry class was held was already full of kids, but the desk up at the front of the room was empty. "I don't know," she said. "I hope they haven't forgotten us!"

"Me too," the girl said, sighing dreamily. "I don't want to miss a minute of this!"

"Me neither." Elizabeth smiled and turned to face her, closing the collection of poems she'd brought from home. "Who's your favorite Romantic poet, anyway?"

"Oh any poet." The girl waved her hand in the air carelessly. "As long as the poem's really romantic. And as long as the guy who wrote it is really foxy."

Foxy? Elizabeth frowned. "Well, like, how do you feel about Keats?" she asked.

"Keats?" The girl looked blank. "What are Keats?"

"You know, John Keats?" Elizabeth asked. The girl shook her head.

How could anybody sign up for Romantic Poetry and not know about Keats? Elizabeth tried again. "Wordsworth? Lord Byron? Longfellow?"

"Long who?" The girl made a face. "Are they your boyfriends or something? I'm talking about *romantic* poetry. You know, like this." She scrabbled in her purse and drew out a greeting card. "My boyfriend sent me this one last week. Check it out."

Elizabeth took the card and opened it. "My Darling," it said in big red cursive letters at the top.

"'Snow isn't purer than your heart/A flower isn't brighter than your face,'" she read aloud.

"Isn't it cool?" the girl said, smiling.

"Cool" wasn't the word Elizabeth would have used. "'I know I've gotten shot by Cupid's dart,'" she went on, "'so now I want to hold you in a fond embrace.'" The card was signed "Love Always, Marty." She gave the girl a weak smile. "It's very nice," she said, "but, um . . . " Was there a nice way of telling her she was in the wrong class? "Um, Romantic poetry is more like, you know, 'Why should the beautiful hide their heads/Why must the beautiful die?'" she quoted.

"Die?" The girl looked incredulous. "What's dying got to do with love? I read, like, five romance novels a week, and the beautiful people never die. Only the villains." She rummaged in her purse again. "Wait till you see the poem my other boyfriend sent me. His stuff doesn't have the same zing as Marty's, but his rhymes are better."

Elizabeth sighed. "Um . . . ," she began.

"Welcome to Romantic Poetry," a slightly familiar voice interrupted. "If I could have your attention? My name is Ethan Williams, and I'll be teaching this class."

Elizabeth jerked her head up and stared at the front of the room. While she had been talking to the other girl, the teacher had come in.

Only . . . he couldn't have been the teacher.

Because she was positive that he was the

same kid she'd run into on the footbridge the night before!

"I hope no one is taking this course in hopes of getting an easy *A*," the ceramics teacher said. "This class is known as one of the most difficult on campus."

Great. Jessica groaned.

But how hard could it be? a little voice in her head told her. Clay was clay. Art was art. It wasn't something you could, like, grade.

"To pass the course—and I emphasize the word 'pass,'" the teacher said, stroking his mustache, "you must complete these following projects to my satisfaction. A plate, two bowls, two pots, three mugs . . . "

Great. Jessica groaned louder. With any luck, there'd be a funky little craft store in the mall. Maybe she'd just go buy what she needed.

"But first," the teacher said in a lilting voice, "we learn how to throw a pot."

Cool, Jessica thought. She wondered why anybody would want to throw the pot after they'd made it. It would probably break, especially if they'd only made it out of clay. Maybe throwing it was, like, a way of testing it to see if it was any good. She leaned forward eagerly.

"By 'throw a pot,'" the teacher said, heaping a pile of clay onto the potter's wheel, "I mean, of course, to make one."

Of course. Jessica sat back with a sigh. What was

the fun of that? Still, she watched with interest as the teacher started to turn the lump of clay into a pot. The potter's wheel was big and flat and spun around like a CD. The teacher's foot pumped up and down; the faster he pumped, Jessica observed, the faster the wheel went. Jessica itched to try it. It looked like fun.

"Now observe," the teacher said. He put his hands into the clay and spun the wheel faster. His fingers moved gently, molding and shaping the clay. Little lumps sheared off the blob in the middle. In a couple of minutes, what was left was already taking on the form of a small bowl.

Awesome, Jessica thought, nodding to herself. What a great idea. You just put your hands there, and the wheel does all the work. Maybe she could adapt the potter's wheel to other parts of life. Like doing math homework, say. Or putting away dishes.

The wheel slowed. "This is the basic outline," the teacher explained. "Many other refinements are possible, naturally. Are there questions so far?"

"It looks fun," a guy in a purple T-shirt commented.

"It looks easy." Jessica was a little startled to hear the words come from her mouth.

"Easy?" The teacher looked over the tops of his spectacles at Jessica. "Have you ever thrown a pot before, young lady?"

Jessica shook her head. "I made, like, a coil pot

in fourth-grade art class. But I'm sure it's easy. All you do is hold your hands a certain way, right? And pump."

The teacher seemed to be holding back a laugh. "If it is that easy, please come demonstrate."

Why not? Jessica thought, looking around at the guys in the classroom. Jessica was never one to shy away from the center of attention, especially not the center of male attention. She stood and walked to the front of the room. "Sure," she said. "Let's get started!"

"*You're* the teacher?" The girl next to Elizabeth sounded unbelieving.

Ethan turned faintly pink. "You're thinking I look kind of young, right?"

"Uh-huh," the girl said dryly. "All my boyfriends look older than you, and they're still in high school."

Ethan smiled. "Well," he said evenly, "during the academic year I'm a student here at SVU. But I'm also a TA, teaching assistant, and part of what I do is teach enrichment classes like this when summer comes around." His eyes swept through the room. "I'm pleased to see all of you . . . here . . . "

Was that a flash of recognition as Ethan looked at her? Elizabeth thought so. She scrunched down in her seat, excited and embarrassed at the same time.

Of course it had been Ethan last night. Who else

would go around quoting Longfellow at her, but the teacher of a poetry class? Anyway, Ethan looked just like the guy at the bridge—the hair, the eyes, even the toothy smile. It was just that—that he'd looked so young last night.

Well, for that matter, he looked awfully young today too. It was hard to believe that he was already a college student. How old did you have to be to be in college? Eighteen, right? Maybe nineteen. Elizabeth frowned. Ethan sure didn't look eighteen.

"There are several important themes in Romantic poetry," Ethan was saying, writing on the chalkboard. "The theme of the *individual*—that people are different from each other. The theme of *connection*—that relationships are important. And, finally—" He grinned that toothy smile again. "—the theme of *nature*. The Romantics were very big on the natural world."

Elizabeth stared at the chalkboard without really seeing it. What a shame that Ethan was so much older. If he was going to be eighteen, or older, getting to know him was clearly out.

The girl next to Elizabeth raised her hand. "When are we going to start talking about love?" she wanted to know.

Love. Elizabeth's heart gave a lurch.

Ethan grinned. "A lot of Romantic poems do deal with love," he said. "But often the love theme is hidden, or it's just a symbol for something else."

He held up a warning finger. "In Romantic poetry, things are seldom what they seem."

Elizabeth blinked. An idea was forming in her mind.

Last night, in the darkness, she'd mistaken Ethan for somebody younger than he was. "Things are seldom what they seem," she repeated to herself.

Well—was there a way to do that same process in reverse?

Was there a way to make Ethan think that she was a lot older than she was?

She stared at the ceiling, half listening to Ethan's voice as he read William Blake's poem "Tyger! tyger! burning bright" aloud.

She knew that trying to fool Ethan wasn't typical Elizabeth behavior.

But, as she'd thought before, college sort of gave you permission to be somebody different. . . .

"Like this?" Jessica asked confidently. She took a giant gob of clay and tossed it onto the top of the potter's wheel.

"Not so much," her teacher suggested. He pulled off a hunk and threw it aside. "You make a small pot, after all, not a ten-gallon wastebasket."

Several students laughed. Jessica set the clay in the center of the wheel the way her teacher had done. Then she held her hands loosely on top of the mound and stepped on the pedal.

Nothing happened.

"Push harder," the teacher suggested, a twinkle in his eye. "It requires a certain amount of strength."

Strength? Jessica frowned. Who did the teacher think she was? Of *course* she was strong. And she certainly wasn't about to come across like a weakling in front of all these guys. Grimacing, she pushed against the pedal even harder.

Still, nothing happened.

"It may take time to get it going," the teacher explained helpfully.

"I know, I know!" Jessica snapped. Maybe it would help if she held the clay down with her fingers. Pushing her hands deep into the wet clay, she stepped on the pedal with all her might and pushed, half rising from her seat. Slowly, the wheel began to turn.

"Yesss!" Jessica exulted. She pumped faster.

"Not so fast!" The teacher stepped quickly forward.

Jessica snorted. After she'd worked this hard, he was telling her to slow down? *I don't think so!* she thought, giving the pedal another kick. The clay did seem to be moving, so she pressed down even more firmly against it—

Shplosh!

Like a sudden reverse tornado, the slick wet clay funneled up between Jessica's fingers. Bits of slimy stuff pelted her face and stuck to her clothes.

"Help!" she shouted—and gagged as a particularly big blob caught her in the mouth.

"I tried to tell you." The teacher sounded amused. "Turning the wheel too fast is a poor idea."

Jessica's foot slid off the pedal. The wheel slowed, but it was too late. She spat out a clump of stringy clay and looked down at her nice new T-shirt through a gray clump hanging from her eyebrow. The T-shirt was stained seven ways from Sunday. Ruined, she thought angrily.

And that wasn't even the worst part, she thought as she stared, embarrassed, out at the class. *The cute guys that she'd been trying to impress?*

All of them were *laughing* at her!

Seven

Why do things like this always have to happen to me? Jessica wondered, exasperated, as she headed down the corridor after ceramics class was over. She'd gone down to the bathroom and cleaned herself up as well as she could after her, um, accident, but her hair was still a mess and there were dark ugly stains all over her T-shirt. Not to mention that her face was downright gross. She didn't think there was really any such makeup as Wet Clay Number Three.

She turned left toward an Exit sign. The guys had laughed themselves sick, and Jessica was sure they wouldn't even talk to her if she saw them around campus. Not that she was going to, if she could help it. She'd hung out in the back of the classroom until everyone else had left, and now the hallway was completely deserted. Jessica breathed a deep, unhappy sigh. Somehow she had the feeling that this wouldn't have happened to Elizabeth.

And that wasn't because Elizabeth was overly-careful or anything either, she told herself with a scowl. It was just that—that whatever Elizabeth did turned out golden, that was all. *Elizabeth* was the one who had wanted to come here to begin with. *Jessica* hadn't. So who got the obnoxious roommate and the clay that exploded? Jessica. Life wasn't fair.

She stopped short as she came to a blank wall. *I must have come the wrong way,* she thought. Frowning, she turned around. Obviously she was in the middle of a gallery of some kind. Display cases hovered nearby in the dim light. Curious, Jessica peered into the nearest one.

Folk Art of the Southwest a sign read. Jessica's eyes flicked across the collection of bowls, masks, and figurines on the top shelf—and came to rest on a weird-looking pot off to the far right. "I could do *that*," she said with a scowl. But her gaze lingered.

The pot looked poorly made, almost childish, with bulges on both sides and a top that didn't seem quite even. Still, there was something about the pot that seemed to pull her in. It was brownish red, with a flared opening and a surprisingly narrow neck. Etched into the side of the pot were strange, unfamiliar symbols. Jessica frowned, wondering what the symbols signified.

Bet it cost, like, five zillion bucks too, Jessica

thought. Face it, she could do better than that with one hand tied behind her back. Well, one finger anyway. If this pot was art, with its lumps and its chicken tracks on the side, well, then the people who decided what art was were stupid idiots. She turned to go find the exit and—

"Oof!" Jessica ducked to the side and put her hands against the wall for support. She had bumped into a short, stooped woman standing almost behind her. Pushing herself back up, she stared at the woman, who was wearing a black and white dress with a black cape. *Weird*, Jessica thought uneasily. No one had been there a moment ago. "Where did you—"

"My apologies, dear." The woman's voice was creaky and old, almost as if it hadn't been used in many weeks. "I didn't realize you were turning around so quickly! Do you like the work in the case?"

"Well—" Jessica wanted to tell the woman that it was pretty stupid, but the thought crossed her mind that perhaps the woman had made some of it herself. "It's—it's interesting," she said lamely.

The woman chuckled as if she knew what Jessica really meant. "But I see you do ceramics yourself, my dear. Come, allow me to present you to some of the college's most treasured possessions." She grasped Jessica's arm with more strength than Jessica would have guessed she'd had. "Look closely at the pot on the far right and tell me what you see."

"On the—far right?" *Well, it looks like a three-year-old made it,* Jessica thought, looking once again at the funny-looking pot at the end of the row. *It's dumb. It's—it's dorky. You couldn't, like, use it for anything. Except maybe drowning ant colonies or something.* But she didn't say that. Instead, she sighed and pretended to be examining it closely. "Fine, um, workmanship," she muttered sarcastically.

"What's that?" the woman asked sharply.

Jessica blinked. "Never—never mind," she said in a strangled tone of voice. As she stared at the pot, the markings seemed to come together before her eyes to form a human face. An oddly twisted face, a face of a person in pain. All at once the markings seemed very realistic. Shivering slightly, Jessica stepped back.

"Ah," the woman said knowingly. "You have seen." She edged closer to Jessica, her black cape smooth and soft in the dim light.

"Wh-What is it?" Jessica half whispered.

The woman's face took on an excited glow. "It is a curse pot," she hissed. Standing almost on tiptoe to reach Jessica's ear, she curled gnarled fingers around her mouth to make a sort of speaking tube. "For getting rid of one's enemies."

Jessica's heart gave a lurch. "Enemies?" she asked. Her whispered voice seemed to bounce off the display case and back at her. She blinked, hoping to see the lines on the pot as just a mishmash once again—but no luck. The face still stared out at her, pleading for help.

"En-em-ies," the woman repeated, drawing out the word. Jessica could feel her hot breath on her cheek. "First, create a pot—any kind will do so long as it's imperfect. Next, etch in the face of the one to be cursed." Her grip tightened on Jessica's shoulder. "Then draw in the evil signs while the clay is still wet. Yes. And when the pot is fired, the spirit of the enemy—"

She paused. Jessica waited, scarcely breathing.

"—the spirit is caught inside the pot," the woman went on with a low throaty laugh, "and the enemy is yours. Just like that poor man, there." She jabbed a stubby forefinger through the air at the display case.

Jessica stared at the pot. She couldn't seem to take her eyes off it. As if in a daze she felt the woman release her arm. Slowly Jessica took another step back, then another and another. The pot was evil, she sensed. She could actually feel evil vibrations coming from it. She swallowed hard. *Who was that man?* she wanted to ask, but the words wouldn't leave her throat. *And— and who trapped his spirit inside the pot? And—*

She squeezed her eyes shut tight. With a huge effort, she turned away from the case and that pot of evil. "What—what happened to him?" she asked, her voice sounding heavy and not like her own at all.

But there was no answer.

And when she opened her eyes again, the woman was gone.

Almost as if she'd never been there at all.

*   *   *

"So—if a person, like, wanted to disguise themselves," Elizabeth said slowly, "how would they go about doing it?"

She sat cross-legged on Marion's bed, a small notepad concealed behind her left leg. She didn't mind picking her roommate's brain, but she did mind having Marion find out what she was doing.

Marion was at her usual position at her desk, thumbing happily through criminology books. "Well, it depends," she said. "Changing clothes is key. Figure out what this other person wears, and go buy some of it, and you're halfway home."

Elizabeth frowned. "I mean, for example, if a person wanted to pretend to be a different, made-up person," she said. "Say, if the person didn't really exist, but you wanted to make somebody think that she did. That it did," she added hastily.

Marion rubbed her nose. "That's easier," she said. "Whoever's doing the disguise just has to make sure that the made-up person is different from them. Different clothes, a different age, stuff like that."

"Different age?" Awkwardly, Elizabeth wrote "clothes" on the pad, hoping Marion wouldn't notice. "No problem."

"It also helps to talk differently," Marion said thoughtfully. "If you wanted to be a teenager, you'd say 'like' and 'awesome' and stuff like that, but a college professor probably wouldn't."

"No, he wouldn't," Elizabeth agreed. Ethan's

language had been pretty formal, now that she thought about it. "Diff. words," she wrote on the pad.

"What's that back there?" Marion wanted to know.

"This?" Elizabeth shoved the pad under her knee. "Oh nothing," she lied. "Just a sore spot, um, on my calf muscle." She rubbed her leg, grimacing with pain.

"Oh." Marion highlighted a passage in her book with a big yellow marker. "Then you can stand up straighter if you want to be taller," she went on. "Or slouch if you want to be short. And you drop your voice real deep if you want to imitate a guy," she said, doing it. "Are you trying to disguise yourself as a guy?"

"Me?" Elizabeth tried hard not to turn pink. "Um, no, this isn't for—for me." She stared down at the floor. "Just, you know, for a friend. Yeah, a friend."

"Uh-huh," Marion said, smirking. "And, oh one other thing. If you're really going to do a disguise, make sure you come up with a name. Otherwise, if someone says, 'Hey, Elizabeth!' and you react, it's, like, all over." She rolled her eyes. "Your disguise is shot to pieces, it's *meat*. You have to know your name and you have to answer to it." She tapped the marker on the book and stared daggers at Elizabeth.

"Oh," Elizabeth said. Could she edge that pad

out without being seen? Probably not. "So, my friend should call herself—" She hesitated. What would be a good name for an older kid? Cool, mature . . . and sort of romantic. "—Like, Geraldine?" she asked tentatively. Geraldine sounded pretty romantic.

"Sure, Geraldine's fine." Marion gave a shrug. "Unless her name is Geraldine."

"It—it isn't." Elizabeth wished she was a better liar. "Um—thanks, Marion," she said brightly. *Geraldine, Geraldine,* she repeated slowly. *My name is Geraldine.* "If you get more ideas, let me, I mean my friend, know, OK?" *Geraldine, Geraldine, Geraldine. Geraldine Wakefield.* The name had a nice ring to it.

"Hey, Geraldine," Marion said softly.

"What?" Elizabeth jerked her head up. "I mean—did you say something?"

Marion grinned. "What exactly are you up to?" she asked.

"Me?" Elizabeth put her hand to her chest in alarm. "What makes you think I'm up to anything?"

Jessica's heart hammered. This was too crazy. She blinked, expecting to see the old stoop-shouldered woman lurking somewhere in the shadows, but there was no one to be seen. "Hello?" she called uncertainly.

No answer.

"Hello?" Jessica tried again, a little louder.

Still there was no answer.

All at once Jessica knew she needed people. Real people, human people, not funny-looking old ladies who babbled about trapping spirits in pots. She broke into a run, trying to get far from that evil curse pot with the terrible agonized face. . . . Not knowing exactly where she was going, she careened around a corner and then another, picking up speed as she went. Left, right, right again—

Splat!

"Why don't you watch where you're going?" a voice yelled.

Startled, Jessica looked around. Shards of pottery lay across the floor, and a handcart was tipped over against a wall, one wheel lazily spinning. A boy about her own age stood rubbing his knee, an angry look on his face. "Now look what you've done!" he said accusingly.

"I—I'm sorry." Jessica bit her lip. Why weren't there horns or something on the cart so she'd have known it was coming? "I—I didn't see you!"

"Duh hey." The boy righted the cart and shook his head, exhaling loudly. "She comes running around the corner like, like she's being chased by King Kong, and all she can say is 'I didn't see you!'" he finished in a falsetto.

"Well—I didn't!" Jessica breathed in, checking to see if her side was badly hurt. "I'm sorry, but I . . ." Her voice trailed off.

"Like 'sorry' will actually help," the boy said

gloomily. Groaning, he got down on his knees and picked up a couple of broken pieces of pottery. "Do you have any idea how long it took some people to make these things? And then, poof, a dumb kid comes around the corner and they're toast."

Jessica knelt too and scrabbled through the wreckage, swallowing hard. "It's not *that* bad," she said brightly. "There's probably a couple of whole ones floating around somewhere."

The boy snorted and began loading the cart with the broken pieces. "Why don't you just get out of here, huh?"

Jessica stood and walked past the wreckage.

This was rapidly turning out to be the worst day of her life.

Elizabeth stood outside Le Boutique de Très Chic and took a deep breath. Tiny little skirts and long flowing ball gowns shimmered on the dummies in the window. One wore a pair of hot pink slippers with racing stripes, another an impossibly spiky pair of black high heels.

If this is très chic, give me très blah! she told herself, rolling her eyes. No way would you get Elizabeth Wakefield into clothes that looked like that.

But that was the point, wasn't it? Elizabeth chewed her lip thoughtfully. Because, after all . . . she wasn't here to be Elizabeth Wakefield. She was here to be somebody else. Somebody . . . older.

Named Geraldine Wakefield. Who might just wear the *très* chicest clothes in Sweet Valley.

Elizabeth glanced furtively around to see if anyone she knew was standing nearby. No one was.

Just do it, she told herself. If her plan was going to work, she'd have to ditch the real Elizabeth and replace her with Geraldine. She'd already worked out a couple of expressions that Geraldine would say a lot: "My, my!" and "Indeed!" And she'd wrinkle her nose a lot too. Elizabeth watched her reflection in the windowpane wrinkle its nose. The real Elizabeth never wrinkled her own nose. Hardly ever anyway.

So what was the holdup? *Just do it!* But Elizabeth's legs wouldn't obey.

"My, my!" she said aloud, trying to get herself into the right frame of mind. "One of my stockings has a run in it and Très Chic is the only place I can get a replacement! Indeed!" She wrinkled her nose. It was now or never.

"Geraldine" Wakefield's hand reached out and swung open the door. *My, my!* she thought, walking into the store and hoping no one had recognized her.

Indeed!

"What happened to *you?*" Susan said, her mouth twisted into an unpleasant grin. "Did you bathe in the clay instead of making a pot?"

"Shut up, Susan." Jessica savagely pulled a

drawer open, looking for a new set of clothes.

"Temper, temper," Susan replied. "Of course, bathing in clay is popular in certain, um, *primitive* cultures, I understand. . . ." She gave an elaborate shrug. "Sweet Valley might qualify. It's certainly an improvement on your usual beauty secrets."

"Walk west till your hat floats." Jessica hated Susan worse than ever. She hated everything about Susan. Her hair. Her so-called smile. Her oh-so-stylish shoes and her fashionable little skirts.

Susan folded her arms. "You're not going to take a shower, are you? You'd just clog up the drains." Laughing hysterically, she got up and waltzed off toward the door. "Bet you were trying to impress some guys with your new outfit, huh, Jess?"

Jessica stuck her fingers in her ears, but the sound of Susan's bright laughter seemed to linger even after she was out of sight.

This is the worst, Jessica thought. She took a deep breath, wishing she'd never come. Wishing she'd gone camping with her parents. Wishing the stupid letter from SVU had never come. . . .

And all at once she was yanking open drawers, pulling her things out and packing them into duffel bags without even bothering to fold them.

Forget changing clothes. She had better things to do.

Like running away.

"Oh you'll love these, dear," the salesclerk said, reaching for a pair of pink heart-shaped earrings.

"The very thing for a chic eighteen-year-old—you did say you were eighteen?"

Elizabeth considered. Already it was hard to keep track of "Geraldine" and her life. "Eighteen, yes," she agreed, standing as tall as possible, and then added "Indeed."

"You don't look eighteen," the woman observed, holding the earrings up to Elizabeth's earlobe.

The earrings looked perfectly disgusting, Elizabeth thought, but Geraldine might like them. "Yeah—I mean, indeed," she replied, wrinkling her nose for good measure. "Everybody says that. That's one of the reasons I want the earrings," she went on. "To make myself look older. My, my."

"Very good," the saleslady said. "So far we have an, er, *grown-up* dress, some cosmetics, and earrings. Heavy date?" she asked with a smile.

Elizabeth didn't smile back. "I hope so," she admitted, wrinkling her nose in a decidedly Geraldine-like way. "Now, some shoes, please."

"Certainly! Have a seat." The saleslady motioned Elizabeth to a chair. "High heels or racing stripes? They're both all the rage these days."

"Heels," Elizabeth said weakly, swallowing hard. She'd scarcely ever worn them.

But it was a good bet that Geraldine had.

Crumb. Jessica sighed. This was the worst day *ever*. Now she'd arrived at the bus stop too late to catch the only bus that went to her neighborhood, and the next one wouldn't be along for three hours. If Sweet Valley only had decent bus service . . .

Gritting her teeth, she started walking down the street. Maybe she'd call Lila and ask her to send a limo to pick her up. She'd already sort of decided to stay with Lila anyway. After all, Lila had offered. Head down, she stomped her way past an ice cream parlor, a pizza joint, a couple of boring old bookstores. Dullsville. Maybe Susan was right. Maybe Sweet Valley was a cultural wasteland, after all.

Unless . . .

Jessica's head snapped up. Le Boutique de Très Chic, she read. Now even Susan would appreciate this. And judging by the stuff in the window, it wasn't bad. The heels weren't exactly Jessica's style, but it'd be a good place to browse, anyway, while she waited for Lila's limo—

Jessica stiffened.

Through the window she could see someone— familiar.

Someone wearing high heels and what Jessica could only describe as a grown-up dress. Not to mention a ton of makeup.

Someone wobbling precariously toward the door while a salesclerk waved good-bye.

Jessica's eyes grew big, and she darted out of the doorway.

Forget going home, she told herself.

It would be much more interesting to hang around and see what Elizabeth was up to.

Eight

◇

"Hello," Elizabeth purred, wrinkling her nose and smiling down at Ethan. Her heart was soaring. She'd wobbled all the way from the boutique to the snack bar in hopes of kind of casually running into him, and here he was—first try!

"Hello?" Ethan looked up quizzically. "Do I, um, know you?"

Yesss! Elizabeth resisted pumping her fist into the air. "No, indeed," she said gravely. "But I believe I know you. My, um, sister has spoken of you." Was that too forward? She hoped not. "That is—"

"Your sister?" Ethan broke into his toothy grin. "Oh! I mean—I can guess who your sister is."

"You can?" Elizabeth started in surprise. "That is—my, my."

"You're Elizabeth's sister, right?" Ethan said

eagerly. He struggled to his feet, nearly knocking over his glass in the process. "Elizabeth, um, Wakefield. Her *older* sister," he added, extending his hand.

"That's right!" Elizabeth smiled. "I'm Geraldine." She straightened up to her full height and shook Ethan's hand. "Indeed."

"Indeed," Ethan echoed her. He motioned to the table. "Have a seat, um—Geraldine."

"Thank you so much," Elizabeth said, gratefully sinking into the chair. "I'm eighteen, by the way."

"I see." Ethan rubbed his nose. "Well, pleased to meet you, Geraldine," he said. "Your, um, sister is quite a kid."

"Oh indeed," Elizabeth said, nodding. "She just loves your class," she went on, casually waving an arm in the air. "Poetry is practically her life, you know."

"Really?" Ethan leaned closer and rested his arms on the tabletop. "I know she reads a lot. Does she, um, like to write poetry too?"

"Indeed" was getting a little old, so Elizabeth just smiled. Anyway, it was time to get Ethan thinking about Geraldine. "She does," she admitted, "but so do I." She wrinkled her nose and giggled, hoping the giggle wouldn't remind Ethan of the kid in his poetry class.

Ethan raised his eyebrows. "So do I, but it's not very good," he admitted, running his hand through his short hair. "I bet Elizabeth's is, like, better than mine."

"Like?" What kind of word is that for an English teacher to use? Elizabeth leaned forward and oh-so-casually bumped her elbow against Ethan's. "Elizabeth's is OK," she said, "but mine is really quite good, if I say so myself." She gave a discreet cough. "Perhaps you'd like to see it sometime."

It was a good thing she was wearing plenty of rouge, Elizabeth decided. Underneath it all she was positive she was blushing up a storm. No way in the world would the real Elizabeth Wakefield have come on that strong. It was kind of fun playing Geraldine—even if Elizabeth wished that Ethan would stop trying to turn the conversation to her and away from, um, Geraldine.

Ethan took a swig of pop and set his glass down with a thump. "Perhaps," he agreed. "And maybe you could bring along some of your sister's work too?"

"Of course," Elizabeth said, nodding. It was a small price to pay; she'd just whip out a few lines that weren't very good and say they were her—Geraldine's—sister's. She frowned and wrinkled her nose. Keeping her personas apart wasn't easy. "Well, when are you free? Tomorrow night?"

Ethan made a face. "Tomorrow night's no good, I'm afraid. Faculty meeting."

"My, my." Elizabeth chuckled. "They keep you coming and going, don't they! Well, what about the next night—Wednesday?"

Ethan stared up at the ceiling. "Sure, Geraldine.

Tell you what, though. Why don't you bring Elizabeth along too? Not just her poetry, but her, in person. I'd like to have a chance to meet her away from the formalities of English class." He laughed easily.

"Um—" Geraldine Wakefield was flustered. Producing Elizabeth's poetry would be hard enough, but producing Elizabeth would be downright impossible. "Um—I'm afraid that won't work."

"Oh." Ethan looked disappointed. "Um—can I ask why not?"

Elizabeth wrinkled her nose. "Family reasons," she said sadly.

"Oh," Ethan said again. Shrugging, he raised his glass again and smiled. "Well—tell her I said hello, anyway, OK?"

"Indeed," Elizabeth said, sliding back out of her seat and stumbling instantly forward. Balancing on high heels was for the birds. "Wednesday night, then. Here."

"Here," Ethan echoed with a wave.

Elizabeth tottered away, trying not to fall. She breathed deeply. That had gone pretty well. It was just weird how Ethan had wanted to have Elizabeth come along. Wouldn't that make it less like a date and more like—well, more like family time?

Elizabeth maneuvered around a table where three girls sat listening dreamily to a love song on the radio.

Or maybe, she thought, stealing a look back at the girls, *maybe Ethan* wants *it to be less like a date. Maybe he's, like, embarrassed. Maybe he's shy and almost afraid of someone who's mature like, um, Geraldine.*

Yeah. That would explain a bunch of things.

Elizabeth sighed. Obviously "Geraldine" was going to have to work hard to get Ethan to feel at ease around her.

Jessica trailed closely behind her sister as she made her way up the steps of Woodbridge Hall. Whatever was going on was totally bizarre. Here was Elizabeth spending, like, three-quarters of her life savings on fancy clothes that she wouldn't usually have been caught dead in, and wandering around the campus in high heels, and meeting some guy in a snack bar, and—

Elizabeth flung the door open with a firm hand. In a flash Jessica was on her. "OK, what are you up to?" she demanded.

Whirling, Elizabeth gasped. "Jess!" she burst out. "I—I—you scared me!"

"Someday I'll give you a lesson in how to wear high heels," Jessica said. "You look like a doofus. And as for that makeup, well . . . " She left the sentence unfinished. "But seriously, Lizzie," she went on, giving her sister a hard glare, "what's up? What's with the getup? And who's the guy in the snack bar, huh?"

Elizabeth drew herself up to her tallest height and scowled down at Jessica. "I'm not going to tell you," she said simply, and with that she wobbled through the door and toward the stairway.

"Hey!" Jessica called to her back, but Elizabeth didn't even turn around.

Not going to tell me! Jessica rubbed her eyes in disbelief. *Since when did Elizabeth get so much— courage, so much backbone?*

It's almost like she's a different person, or something! she thought irritably.

"This is very nice," Jessica's ceramics teacher told her gravely the next morning. He held up the pot Jessica had made and displayed it for the class to see. "I suppose you have now learned how much pressure to put on the wheel."

"I suppose so," Jessica agreed, trying not to grin too much. It hadn't been easy, but she'd mastered the technique of pumping at just the right speed— and the pot she'd thrown that morning had been only a little lumpy. "Thanks."

"Now decorate it," the teacher told her, pointing to a nearby table. "Sticks, wires—any tool will do so long as it digs in evenly and smoothly."

"Sure." Jessica carried her pot gently to the table, remembering how the pots had shattered when she'd run into that guy with the cart yesterday. It wouldn't do to smash this one. Her thoughts drifted back to the cute guy who'd been piloting the cart, and then to that old woman in the gallery, with the . . . what had she called it?

The curse pot.

Jessica sat still, picturing that pot in her mind. In a strange way, she could see a resemblance between her pot and that one. Though hers was less lopsided, of course. It was hard to believe she'd taken the idea of the curse seriously. In the dim light of the gallery, with that crazy lady cackling like a witch, it had been pretty spooky, but out here—well, it was funny.

And suddenly she had an idea.

Just for yucks, she'd put Susan's picture into her pot. Yeah. Susan was still acting incredibly rude. That morning she'd asked Jessica if she was going to go play with the pigs again. Then she'd held her nose and said something about picking a truly cool roommate "next time." Jessica's eyes flashed. Well, if curse pots actually existed, she couldn't think of any better victim than Susan "the Pill" Rainer.

Let's see—curving cheekbone, long hair parted at the side . . . Jessica grinned as she found a penknife and began to dig into the wet clay.

"Elizabeth—before you leave, could I see you for a moment?"

Elizabeth stopped on her way out the door of the poetry class, surprised and delighted to hear Ethan speaking. "What is it?" she asked, coming and standing next to Ethan's desk.

Ethan smiled shyly. "Mostly, I wanted to compliment you on your first essay." He scuffed the toe of his sneaker into the wooden floor. "It's not every day that I meet someone your age with so much insight into works like these."

Elizabeth's heart leaped. "Indeed?" she started to say, but then covered it up with a cough. After all, she wasn't Geraldine now. "I mean—thank you."

"Thank you." Ethan grinned. "Without you, this class would be like pulling teeth. I'm really impressed, I mean it. Have you considered, you know, an academic career? There's not much of a market for English professors, but . . ." He broke off. "Of course, it's a long way before you have to think about it yet."

Elizabeth wondered why Ethan sounded so down. "I was thinking about journalism," she answered honestly. "But maybe—"

"Anyway," Ethan continued quickly. "I don't know if she told you, but I ran into your sister yesterday?"

Elizabeth raised her eyebrows. "You mean Jess—that is, Geraldine?"

"Geraldine," Ethan agreed. "You have, um, two sisters?"

"Two." Elizabeth slouched a little, trying to appear shorter, just in case Ethan noticed an especially strong family resemblance. "Jessica's my age. We're twins, and Geraldine's older. Yes, she spoke to me about meeting you," she lied. "She said she thought you were kind of cool."

"Kind of cool?" Ethan chuckled. "Story of my life, Elizabeth. Kind of cool." He leaned against the blackboard. "Oh, Ethan," he said, waving his hand dismissively in the air. "He's *kind* of cool. But not very."

"Oh—I didn't mean—" Elizabeth bit her lip. "I mean, she didn't mean . . ." She tried again. "When Geraldine says 'kind of cool,' she means what most people would mean if they said 'really cool.'"

Ethan smiled faintly. "Anyway," he went on, "I'd said I'd meet her for a cup of coffee tomorrow night, and I'd wanted, you know, you to come along too, and . . ." His voice trailed off. "She said you were busy, but I thought it was worth a try. Did you, like, have a change of plans since then?" His eyes were hopeful.

"Oh." Elizabeth stepped back. "No, Ethan, I'm—sorry. I really am busy." Swinging her backpack onto her shoulder, she dashed from the room. "See you tomorrow!" she called out.

Once as myself—and once as Geraldine!

Jessica went into the hall, whistling. She'd stayed late in ceramics class to finish decorating her pot, and it was pretty cool even if she did say so herself. Not that she was the greatest artist in the world or anything, but you could tell it was Susan's face all right. She'd drawn her in the act of rolling her eyes, which was how she usually saw Susan. It was a miracle Susan's eyes didn't roll right out of her head.

The hallway was deserted, and Jessica walked with a spring in her step. It was fun to tell Susan off like this. She rounded the corner—and came face-to-face with the guy she'd run into the day before.

"Uh-oh" he said, flattening himself against the wall in mock alarm. "It's the Human Tornado!"

"Yeah, well, if you'd just stayed on your side of the road—," Jessica began. But her mood was too good to stay sour. "I'm sorry," she said shyly, dropping her gaze.

"Hey. So am I," the boy admitted. "I—I really went ballistic, and I, like, shouldn't have. I mean, it's only clay."

Jessica shrugged. "Yeah, but it was people's work, wasn't it?"

The boy winked. "Not very good work," he told her. "Some of it—well, it was just as well that it busted, if you catch my drift."

Jessica laughed. "My name's Jessica," she said, extending her hand. He was pretty cute, she decided—tall and wiry, with longish hair and a freckled face that made him seem a little like a cowboy.

"Bernard," the boy said, shaking her hand. "Listen. I was on my way to load more stuff into the kiln. Want to come?"

Jessica frowned. "The kiln's where you, like, roast them, right?"

"You could say that." The boy laughed. "It's a big oven, pretty much. You cook 'em at a certain temperature for a nice long time, and they dry out.

Then you can drink out of 'em, and they won't fall apart anymore—though they will shatter if you throw 'em around," he added, looking directly at Jessica, who blushed. "So how about it?"

Jessica had a sudden picture of her pot being loaded into the flames, with Susan's face twisted in agony. *"No, no, no!" Susan's spirit would shout, trapped inside the pot, but Jessica would laugh like a mad scientist and shove the pot into the kiln, which would be heated to six thousand degrees. And Susan would be gone forever . . .*

She nodded. "You bet!" she told Bernard.

Nine

◇

"You know, even the food here is pretty decent," Elizabeth said. It was dinnertime, and she was seated at a cafeteria table with Jessica and Marion. She sipped her soup.

"Way better than the so-called food they give us at school," Jessica agreed. Ketchup trickled down her chin. "At school the burgers are so small you need, like, a microscope to tell they're on your plate."

"You guys should come to my school," Marion said lazily, pushing tomato slices around her salad bowl. "We have the *worst*. There's tuna surprise, except the only one surprised was the tuna, and mushroom noodle casserole, which looks like barf and tastes the same. And every Tuesday they serve lima beans and cauliflower."

"Ga-ross." Jessica speared a french fry. "You should see the grilled cheese sandwiches our cook makes. They have so little cheese we called them grilled cheese wannabes."

Elizabeth put down her spoon. "So where's Susan?" she wanted to know.

"IDK and IDC," Jessica said smugly.

"Talk English, please," Marion said.

"IDK means I don't know," Jessica explained, "and IDC means I don't care. And I *don't*." Susan hadn't shown up all afternoon, which had made Jessica one happy camper. She sipped her milk and grinned. With any luck Susan was lying bruised and bleeding at the bottom of a cliff somewhere.

Well . . . that sounded a little harsh. Maybe bruised and bleeding at the bottom of a flight of stairs instead.

Elizabeth looked around the dining hall. "It seems a little emptier tonight. Or is it just my imagination?"

"No, it's emptier," Marion assured her. "The Nature Scouts all went on a canoeing trip. They'll be gone till Friday."

Jessica raised her eyebrows. "How do you know?"

Marion smiled wickedly. "Oh I have my ways. When you're an accomplished detective like me, it's a snap."

"Yeah?" Elizabeth looked curiously at Marion. "What did you do, pay tens and twenties for information?"

"Put on a disguise and infiltrate the group?" Jessica asked. She had once seen a movie where a cop had done exactly that.

"A good detective is like a magician—she never reveals her secrets." Marion buttered a roll. "But for you I'll make an exception." She dropped her voice to a whisper. "There was a list of events outside the cafeteria door. And I *read it*."

Jessica laughed and set down her glass. "I guess detective work is just doing the obvious sometimes," she said.

"Hey, haven't we, um, *run* into each other somewhere before?"

Jessica looked up to see Bernard, the kiln guy, standing next to her with a heavily loaded tray. He winked at her. "*Run*, get it? Mind if I sit down?" he asked.

"Sure." Jessica couldn't help groaning at his awful pun, but she slid over to make room for him. She introduced him to Elizabeth and Marion. Funny how he looked cuter than ever. "It's, um, nice to see you again," she said, trying not to blush.

"Nice to see you." Bernard grabbed the salt shaker and sprinkled salt on his fries. "Hey, I was pulling stuff out of the kiln, and your pot looks truly awesome."

Awesome? Jessica sat up straight, wondering if she'd heard correctly. "Um—awesome?" she said shyly.

"Yeah, awesome," Bernard replied between bites

of hamburger. "That face on the outside? It's, like, totally evil."

"Evil?" Elizabeth looked quizzically at her sister.

"Yeah, evil," Jessica replied. "It wasn't hard to do. When you have a roommate like I have . . ." She shrugged elaborately.

It was strange, she thought happily. Just twenty-four hours earlier she'd almost run away. Now her point of view had changed one hundred percent. She'd met Bernard, she'd beaten the potter's wheel. Dinner was tasty, and Susan was gone.

She hummed to herself, watching Bernard eat. All she had to do was find out what Elizabeth was up to with the fancy clothes, and she'd be golden.

"So, you're really enjoying this Romantic poetry class," Marion said to Elizabeth as they climbed the hill back to Woodbridge Hall after dinner.

Elizabeth nodded vigorously. "You could say that." *Actually, that would be the understatement of the century*, she told herself. Poetry, and the Romantics too, and of course Ethan, who was really cute. In an older kind of way, of course.

"Cool," Marion said happily. "Today we learned about catching suspects off guard. It's really useful. Remember in Christine Davenport book 45, when Christine calls the villain on the phone and pretends she's, like, selling storm windows, and then she says, 'Oh by the way, Mr. Sneed, why did you try to murder your wife and kids and even the cat?'

and he was so flummoxed he just said 'Hey—how did *you* know about that?' And so they arrested him? Remember?"

Elizabeth tore her thoughts away from Ethan. "Book 45 was pretty decent."

"Yeah. Well anyway, that's the kind of thing we learned," Marion said carelessly. "Only more up-to-date, of course. You can get people to reveal a lot about themselves with a well-placed question."

"Uh-huh." Elizabeth's mind drifted back to Ethan again. It was funny how real his face seemed to be in her thoughts. Almost as if she could reach out and touch it.

"Like, I'll give you a for instance," Marion went on. She whirled to face Elizabeth. "Who's Geraldine trying to impress?" she hissed.

"Ethan," Elizabeth said automatically. "I mean—that is . . . wait a minute . . ." Trying hard to save the situation, she stared at Marion and shook her head. "Geraldine? Geraldine who?"

"Ethan, huh?" Marion winked at Elizabeth. "Piece of advice, kid. Don't ever try to fool a great detective!"

"You know, she never came back last night," Jessica said thoughtfully. It was early the next morning, and the twins were walking down the hill that led from the dining hall to their classes.

"Really?" Elizabeth frowned. "Who didn't come back where?"

"Susan, doofus," Jessica snapped. "Who else? When I went to sleep, her bed was empty. When I woke up in the morning, her bed was still empty."

Elizabeth scratched the back of her neck. "Maybe she's, like, an early riser?"

"No way." Jessica shook her head so hard she could almost hear her skull rattle. "The bed was made. And I didn't sleep late either."

"Hmm." Elizabeth turned onto a grassy path. "That does sound kind of weird."

"Do you think I should, you know, tell the RA or somebody?" Jessica hoped Elizabeth would say no. "I mean, she's a big girl, right? She can take care of herself. It's just that . . ." *Just that . . . just that I don't know exactly why, but I'm a little worried about her,* she thought. *Just that I feel responsible if something . . . happened.*

But that was silly, of course.

Elizabeth smiled. "Know what I bet? I bet she found a slumber party going on in some other room and stayed over there instead."

Jessica nodded slowly. "Yeah," she said, liking the idea. "And if we're lucky, she'll stay there for good!"

"Hey. What did I tell you?" Bernard asked, triumph in his voice.

Jessica's class had just ended, and Bernard had wheeled the students' finished and fired work back into the classroom. He held up Jessica's pot. "Cool, huh?" he asked, turning it this way and that.

Jessica caught her breath. "Cool" didn't even begin to describe it. The pot was about a million percent improved from before it had gone into the kiln. The grayish clay had hardened into a lustrous silver. Light seemed to dance around the curves of the pot. Even the lumps appeared to have flattened out.

But the designs etched into the side of the pot had changed the most. They stood out radiantly from the surrounding colors. In fact, the face was the first thing that caught Jessica's eye. Jessica felt a sense of pride. She'd done it. She'd captured Susan's expression, using only a pocketknife and clay. No matter which way Bernard held the pot, there was no mistaking the face. "Cool," she agreed, finding her voice.

Slowly she reached out to touch the pot. The top was smooth, the sides cold and hard and rough where the knife had hewed out little furrows in the clay. It was awesome to think that she could have actually *made* this.

"What are you planning to use it for?" Bernard wanted to know. "The great thing about pottery is you can do stuff with it. Not like *most* kinds of art. You can cook in it, eat out of it, put flowers in it, wear it for a hat . . ."

"I—I don't know yet." There was something truly fascinating about the pot. With difficulty Jessica tore her eyes away. "What did you have in mind?" she asked.

"Oh, nothing." Bernard shrugged, his long hair cascading across his collar. "But what I really had in mind was, you know, eating. It's been *years* since breakfast." He rested a hand on Jessica's shoulder. "How about it? Want to do lunch?"

"I'll be seeing your sister tonight." Ethan stood over Elizabeth, smiling. Class had just ended, and Elizabeth was gathering together her notebooks. "Sure we can't convince you to join us?"

Elizabeth swallowed hard. "I'm sorry, Ethan." She picked up a book and stuffed it into her backpack. "I hope you, um, have fun tonight."

"Oh we will," Ethan said. But he didn't take his eyes off Elizabeth.

"You'll love Geraldine," Elizabeth said, feeling her heart race. "She's, like, totally cool, and she really knows about poetry. You guys will get along so well."

Ethan nodded. "She told me she likes poems a lot," he said, running his hand through his hair. "Don't tell her I said so, Elizabeth, but I think you use words that are more, you know, down-to-earth. A lot of people think the Romantics were flowery and wrote fancy-schmantzy poetry with lots of obscure words, but if you look at the time when they were writing and all . . ." He grinned shyly. "End of lecture. Anyway, she says 'My, my!' a lot, and 'Indeed!' even more, and it's hard to imagine her writing good poetry, is all."

Elizabeth felt herself turning red. Maybe she'd laid on the 'My, my!' stuff a little thick. "But she *does*," she insisted. "Write good poetry, I mean. Geraldine's shown me a lot of what she's written, and, well . . . I think it's really good."

"If you say so." Ethan's tone grew shy. "I was, um, going to the cafeteria for lunch, even though I only have about half an hour before I have to do some other stuff, and I thought maybe you might—that is, since we're the only ones left, possibly you'd—" He grimaced. "Oh, blast. Want to come to lunch with me?"

Elizabeth was sorely tempted. But she decided she'd better leave the field open for Geraldine. It wouldn't do to have Ethan talk poetry with her all afternoon and then not have anything left over to say to Geraldine. "I'm really sorry, I can't," she said, making a face. "I have something else to do for, like, half an hour."

Waiting for lunch would give her time to work on the poems she'd been writing, anyway. The two poems, to be exact: a good one, by Geraldine, all about a real Romantic hero named Edward, and another not-so-good one, by Elizabeth (the *real* Elizabeth), all about rabbits hopping on a green forest floor. "But you'll see Geraldine tonight," she said cheerfully. "And maybe I'll run into you later on at the cafeteria."

Ethan grinned his toothy grin. "I hope so," he said.

*   *   *

The cafeteria was a madhouse. It was just as well that the Nature Scouts were all gone, Jessica decided, but it felt as if all of Sweet Valley had come for lunch to take the Scouts' places.

She and Bernard were wedged tightly into a corner, sharing a table with about ten other kids, none of whom she knew. There was barely even room to hang her jacket on the back of her chair. So many kids had been in the cafeteria line, she'd gotten jostled around and had wondered if she'd ever find Bernard again. "Is it always like this?" she yelled to Bernard. He'd told her that he had a summer job working in the ceramics building and was taking classes as well, so he'd been around for about three weeks already.

"Usually worse!" Bernard yelled back above the noise of a thousand different conversations.

Jessica grinned. She didn't want to be around it when it got worse!

"Where are you from anyway?" Bernard shouted, spooning applesauce into his mouth.

"Right here in Sweet Valley," Jessica told him, wondering if she should feel embarrassed about it the way she'd felt around Susan.

Bernard's eyes flew wide open. "Cool!" he said excitedly. "I'm from a little burg in the middle of the desert, and I gotta tell you, this is such a happening town!"

Ten

◇

Not a bad day at all, Jessica told herself after dinner that evening. She set the pot up on top of her bookshelf, truly pleased with it. She'd had lunch with Bernard. She'd hit the pool and the mall. And best of all, Susan still wasn't back.

Time to think about the evening ahead of her. She could just kind of casually go for a walk somewhere near the ceramics building and maybe happen to bump into Bernard. If he was still over there. Of course, it was possible he wasn't; he'd told Jessica that he'd made a few friends already while he'd been at SVU. Or she could grab Elizabeth and see if there was a good movie playing at the student union. Or . . . well, there were lots of possibilities. She grabbed her jacket and put it on. Thrusting her hands deep into the pockets, she headed for—

Wait a minute.

Jessica frowned. Some paper was floating around the right-hand pocket of her jacket. But she'd cleaned the pocket just before she'd left for college. She'd had to because of the humongous wad of bubble gum that she'd forgotten about. . . . Her fingers probed the paper.

Strange. It was a sheet of creamy white stationery, neatly folded into quarters. Curious, Jessica tugged it open. "It's—a poem," she murmured, squinting at the sheet. "What's a poem doing in my pocket?"

The sheet contained about fourteen lines, written in red in a beautiful flowing cursive, with the heading "Ode to Blue-Green Eyes." Jessica's heart skipped a beat. "My eyes are bluish green," she said half to herself. She scanned the sheet for the name of the poem's author, but there was none.

"Bernard?" she asked herself in the silence of the room. She turned the paper this way and that. When had she worn the jacket last? At lunch, she decided. And at lunch Bernard had been sitting next to her, with her jacket on the back of her chair. And he'd been to her right, which would have made it easy to drop the poem into her right-hand pocket. A slow smile spread across her face. It had to be Bernard!

Eagerly, she began reading the poem.

O blue-green eyes, that have such wondrous charms!

O hair of gold, O lovely smile so free,
Would that I might find refuge in thy arms
Or, barring that, in mind's embrace with thee. . . .

Jessica's grin widened. She hadn't expected such
fine language from Bernard, but now that she
thought about it, why not? He was artistic, right?
And artistic people had lots of different ways to express themselves. "'O blue-green eyes, that have
such wondrous charms!'" she repeated to herself.

"Knock, knock?"

Quickly Jessica shoved the poem under her pil-
low. "Come in!" she called out.

The door opened, and the Resident Adviser
walked in, papers in her hand. "Hi, Jessica," she
said, smiling. "I hope you're having a good time
here at SVU."

"You could say that," Jessica agreed. *Of course,*
she thought cheerfully, *it would be the understatement of the century.* First the pot, then Bernard, and
now the poem . . .

"Excellent," the RA said. "I was looking for
Susan. Have you seen her lately?"

Jessica frowned. "Actually, no."

"Not since this morning, huh?" The RA's smile
was broad. "Glad to see she's out enjoying herself."

"Well," Jessica tapped her shoe against the
linoleum. "As a matter of fact—"

"Is there a problem?" The RA raised her eyebrows.

"No," Jessica said. "I mean, yes. I mean—" She took a deep breath. Maybe it was time to start all over. "When I came back from class yesterday after lunch," she said slowly, "Susan wasn't here. Her bed was made and everything. And—well—"

"You haven't seen her since yesterday afternoon?" The RA frowned.

Jessica thought hard. "Since yesterday morning."

"Yesterday morning?" The RA's face froze. "You're kidding."

"Um—no," Jessica admitted. "I—I just figured she could take care of herself. See, my sister and I, we—we decided she'd gone to some other room and slept over there . . ." Her voice trailed off.

"Maybe she did." The RA's mouth was a tight line. "Or maybe she's fallen down a flight of stairs or gotten lost in the woods, did you ever think of that?"

Several times, Jessica thought. But all she said was, "Really?"

"Jessica." The RA sighed. "I know you and Susan don't get along, but that's no reason not to tell me she's gone. Probably she's perfectly safe, but *possibly* she's hurt, and if so we need to find her right away." She stared daggers at Jessica. "Do you understand what I'm saying?"

"Uh-huh," Jessica grunted, looking firmly at the floor.

"All right." The RA shook her head. "I need to report this to campus security. If she shows up, send her to me right away. And if she's hurt, well—" She broke off abruptly. But Jessica could fill in the rest of the sentence herself.

The door banged shut. When Jessica looked back up, the RA was gone. "It's not my fault," Jessica said aloud, breaking the silence. "I mean, I—I did what I thought was best." She looked beseechingly at the pot. "And it wasn't just me, it was Elizabeth too! She was the one who—"

All at once she drew in her breath.

The early evening light had changed. A rich, low beam from the sun floated through the window-pane and struck Jessica's pot squarely in the face she'd carved onto it. Not *the* face, she corrected herself. Her mouth suddenly felt dry. Her face. *Susan's* face. Bathed in the glow of the dying sun, it seemed worse than ever. More pained. More tortured. As though the lips were parting to cry a terrible call for help . . .

Jessica swallowed hard. There was a horrible sinking feeling in her stomach. *It can't be*, she told herself. *It—it can't be. The pot's a joke! You can't really put a curse on someone. . . .*

A cloud drifted past the sun. All at once the face changed color. The eyes looked piercingly out toward Jessica. The lips curved into a scream of agony.

Jessica couldn't take it anymore.

"Elizabeth!" she called, darting from the room.

*   *   *

Jessica dashed into the snack bar five minutes later, panting hard. She'd run all the way from Elizabeth's room. Trust her sister not to be there. What had Marion said? *"She's in the snack bar, Jessica. But you probably won't recognize her."* Then she'd laughed uproariously . . . not that Jessica had understood the joke . . .

Jessica blinked in surprise. There was her sister, sitting at a table with some guy, totally glammed out again. If Jessica were in a different frame of mind, she might have hung back, spying on her sister from a distance. But right now, she needed to talk to her. With a gasp of relief, she headed toward the table.

"Elizabeth?" The guy turned to look. Setting down his coffee cup, he grinned at her. "Good to see you!"

"Elizabeth?" Elizabeth said—only her face bore a look of astonishment rather than pleasure.

"Elizabeth?" Jessica skidded to a stop. "What are you—"

"Oh, Elizabeth," Elizabeth said reproachfully. She folded her arms and wrinkled her nose. "What a joker, ha ha ha. I was just showing Ethan, here, some of the poetry you wrote."

Jessica stared from Elizabeth's face to Ethan's and back. *Ethan.* Yeah. He was definitely the guy who'd been with Elizabeth on Monday. Plus, she thought she'd seen him someplace else. Maybe the line at the cafeteria the other day, when she'd gotten

separated from Bernard? *That was it*, she thought—
*he was one of the zillion guys who'd bumped into her
back then.*

"It's pretty decent," Ethan said with a low
chuckle. He couldn't seem to keep his eyes off
Jessica. "I'd have expected a little more sophistica-
tion, maybe, but Geraldine told me it was one of
your, um, earlier works. I really liked the image of
the rabbit huddled under the tree, by the way."

Jessica scratched her head, puzzled. Who was
Geraldine? Why was Elizabeth in this getup? And
what was this about rabbits and 'earlier works,'
anyway? She was about to say something about the
pot when she noticed her sister winking at her
frantically. "Play along," Elizabeth was mouthing.

Play along. Well—why not? "Um—thanks!"
Jessica said brightly. "That was an easy one to
write. Tossed it off in a couple of minutes."

"Really?" Ethan looked surprised.

"She likes to say that." Elizabeth glared at
Jessica. "Actually, the creative process takes a little
longer."

"Whatever." Jessica did feel that Elizabeth's pri-
orities were backward. Wasn't it more impressive
to write a poem all at once than slave over it? Then
you could go watch TV or something afterward.
"Sometimes it's long, and sometimes it's short!"
*And boy oh boy, Lizzie, are you going to owe me big
time when this is all over!*

"Actually, Geraldine," Ethan said, turning to

Elizabeth, "some of the Romantics did write quickly, so Elizabeth's not wrong to write the rabbit one the way she did. Keats, for instance." He smiled at Jessica. "Remember the one we covered in class today? 'On First Looking into Chapman's Homer'? Keats wrote that one in a burst of creativity. Took him ten minutes."

Geraldine. Jessica narrowed her eyes and stared at her sister. So Elizabeth plus oodles of grown-up clothes equaled Geraldine. Interesting.

"Oh I'm sure Elizabeth remembers that poem," Elizabeth said. "Don't you, Lizzie? 'Much have I traveled in the realms of gold,'" she quoted.

"Oh yeah, that one." Jessica laughed, wondering what else to say. "Yeah, I've traveled there too" didn't seem quite right, somehow. "Yeah, that one sure was a hoot," she said instead.

There was a sudden silence. *Oops,* Jessica thought. *Wrong answer.* "I meant to say, so sad," she added quickly. "Such a sad, sad poem. I had, like, big tears in my eyes afterward."

"Oh stop kidding around, Elizabeth," Elizabeth said. Her tone was light, but her teeth were clenched, and there was murder in her eyes. "What she means to say, if she weren't being such a ditz, is that it was such a serious poem. With so many interesting images."

"That too," Jessica said with a shrug.

"Well, I did think your 'Ode to a Rabbit' had some literary merit," Ethan said kindly, running his hand through his hair.

"Oh well, thanks." Jessica saw a chance to redeem herself. "Hey, Geraldine," she said, "know what? I got an ode of my own today. Someone just dropped it into my jacket pocket, can you imagine?"

"Well, of all the nerve!" Ethan said, but he seemed to be holding back a grin. "Was it, um, an ode to something in particular? Like eyes, for example?"

"An Ode to Blue-Green Eyes," Jessica said, nodding. "Listen, guys, don't you just think odes are the greatest?" It was the sort of thing Elizabeth might say. "There's no ode like a great ode, wouldn't you agree, Geraldine?"

"Excuse me, please," Elizabeth said brightly. She stood up, seeming much taller in her high heels. "My, my, Ethan, we'll have to, um, conclude this later if you don't mind. Family problems," she explained.

And the next thing Jessica knew, she was out on the steps of the student union building, with Elizabeth—um, Geraldine—clutching her arm.

"Thanks a *lot*," Elizabeth said bitterly. She took a deep breath. "Thanks for barging in just when things were going well. And thanks for making me into such a doofus!"

"Well, I couldn't help it," Jessica protested. "You didn't give me a script or anything."

"You weren't supposed to need one!" Elizabeth

knew she sounded harsh, but she was angry. "You're *supposed* to have common sense. Romantic poems aren't *supposed* to be a hoot! They're *supposed* to be serious. And besides—" Elizabeth caught herself before her shoes slipped out from under her on the stone step. "Besides, you weren't even *supposed* to be there!"

"Sor-ry," Jessica grumbled. "Listen, I didn't come over here to wreck up your little romance, you know. Or Geraldine's, I mean," she added quickly. "I came over because there's an emergency at the dorm."

"An emergency?" Elizabeth sighed. Somehow, she didn't exactly believe her sister. "Jessica, your whole *life* is an emergency. What makes this any different?"

"It's the pot, Lizzie, the pot I made!" Jessica explained. "It made Susan disappear, somehow—and I need you to help get her back!"

Elizabeth blinked. "OK if I press the rewind button on that?" she asked.

Jessica took a deep breath. "I made a curse pot, for a joke, but Susan hasn't come back, and the RA's worried, and you've got to help me undo the spell!"

Elizabeth frowned. "You put a *spell* on her?"

"Kind of," Jessica admitted. "And you *have* to help! Let's go!" She tugged frantically at her sister's sleeve.

"Jessica." Sometimes Elizabeth found her sister

impossible to understand. "There's no such thing as a curse pot. Or casting a spell. You've known that since, like, second grade. Anyway, how would you undo it?"

Jessica licked her lips. "There was this weird lady at the art gallery. She'd know how. We have to find her. Come on!"

Elizabeth shook her head. "That's crazy and you know it."

"You're saying you refuse?" Jessica looked at her searchingly.

"Darn right I refuse." The last thing Elizabeth wanted to do was to tramp all over town looking for some harmless little old lady who hung out in art galleries.

"OK." A smile played around Jessica's face. "Then I march into the snack bar and tell What's-His-Name all about your little scheme, *Geraldine*."

Elizabeth leaped as if she'd been stung. "You wouldn't dare!"

"Oh wouldn't I?" Jessica said, looking smug.

"You wouldn't," Elizabeth repeated, but she could tell by looking at her sister's face that Jessica meant it, all right. With a sigh, she spread out her hands. She knew when she was beaten. "OK," she agreed after a moment. "But make it quick!"

"You don't really think that old lady's still here, do you?" Elizabeth asked doubtfully.

Jessica looked at the ceramics building, shuttered and dark. "Well," she began. It would be so easy to go back to the dorm and forget about Susan, she told herself. In fact, maybe Susan was even already there. Then she'd feel pretty stupid looking for that dippy woman.

On the other hand, that churning sensation in the pit of her stomach wasn't going away. "We don't really have a choice," she argued.

"What are we going to do?" Elizabeth wanted to know. "Open the door and yell for her? What's her name, anyway?"

"I—I don't know," Jessica admitted. It did seem a little crazy to just yell, as if the woman lived among the display cases.

Elizabeth rolled her eyes. "And for this I left my big date with Ethan," she complained. "So we're going to stick our heads in and yell 'Little old lady!' and someone will yell back 'Little old lady who?' and we'll say—"

Gee, I didn't know you could yodel. Jessica finished the joke glumly in her head. "Maybe there'd be, like, a faculty directory posted on the wall," she said hopefully. The building looked forbidding, silhouetted against the night sky. "Then—"

"But you don't know her name, so the list would have to say 'Little Old Lady,'" Elizabeth cut in. She jiggled the door handle. "Plus, Jess, the door's locked. Go play detective some other night."

"What's this about playing detective?" a familiar

voice asked from the shadows behind them.

"Marion!" Elizabeth whirled around. "Where did you come from?"

"Oh I've just been practicing," Marion said airily. "For my future career. I've been following you guys. You didn't notice, did you?" She stepped out into the light.

"Um—no." Jessica frowned at her sister. Why hadn't Elizabeth known they were being followed? It was a little weird to think that Marion had been hanging on every word since . . . since . . . She turned to Marion. "How long have you been following us?"

Marion grinned. "Since you left my room in hysterics."

Elizabeth clapped a hand to her mouth. "So you saw me and Ethan . . ."

"Hey, no problemo," Marion assured her. "You're not under suspicion for anything, *Geraldine*. I won't give away your secrets. So what's this about playing detective?"

"Well—" Jessica guessed she might as well tell Marion the whole story. Haltingly she explained it all—how Susan had disappeared right after Jessica had made the pot, how the pot had suddenly turned evil, how she needed to get into the building right that very moment . . .

Marion squared her shoulders. "I don't see how it'll help to get in now," she said.

"Yes, it will—because then I can show you the

original curse pot." It made sense, Jessica decided. If Marion and Elizabeth saw the power and the agony in that pot, they'd believe.

"Oh *please*." Elizabeth rolled her eyes.

"No, this sounds cool." Marion stepped forward, a gleam in her eye. "But the door's locked, and I bet the windows are too. Hmm."

"If everything's locked, then we can't go in anyway." Elizabeth pushed gently against a window, which refused to give. "See? Let's go."

"Wait a minute." Marion rummaged in her pockets and pulled out a paper clip. "I'm getting pretty good at picking locks, remember?" Deftly she bent the clip at an angle and inserted it into the lock. Jessica watched eagerly as Marion jiggled the clip this way and that.

"Christine Davenport always uses a skeleton key," Elizabeth pointed out.

"Old-fashioned." Marion was intent on her work. "Anyway, they don't sell skeleton keys to minors." There was a clicking noise, and the door swung silently open. Marion stood back, a note of pride in her voice. "Aha!" she said.

Jessica watched the door opening with a mixture of relief and fear.

Now they could go look for the pot.

But first, they'd actually have to go inside the dark spooky building.

"This is really creepy," Elizabeth said, hoping her voice didn't sound too shaky. In the dim light of the ceramics building, the display cases all looked as if they were about to reach out and grab her.

"I'm almost sure it's this way," Jessica hissed. Marion had already told them that guards probably patrolled the building, so they should keep their voices down. Marion had also brought along a flashlight. "Don't leave home without it," she'd said proudly, turning on the beam and plunging into the darkness with the twins on her heels.

Elizabeth's heart pounded. If there were guards, she was sure they'd be able to hear the sound.

"Left," Jessica commanded. "Now right . . . now straight." She drew in her breath. "There. Feast your eyes."

Marion focused the flashlight beam on a lumpy pot up in the corner. Elizabeth frowned. It didn't look especially interesting, she thought. Just an ordinary, not very good-looking pot with some lines—

She froze. Jessica was right.

The lines weren't random. They formed a face. A horrible face, a face contorted in terrible pain, just as Jessica had said.

"You see it, don't you?" Jessica said sympathetically. She reached out for Elizabeth's shoulder. "Totally gross, huh?"

"I—," Elizabeth began, but the words caught in her throat. "I—"

"Shh!" Marion switched the flashlight off. "Someone's coming! Hide!"

Heart thumping again, Elizabeth darted under a table after Marion and Jessica.

"Hello?" a man's voice called out from somewhere nearby. "Anybody here?"

The girls held their breath. Footsteps came near. A sharp beam of light pierced the darkness.

Don't look down, Elizabeth commanded. She was positive her foot was sticking out, but she didn't dare pull it closer to the rest of her body. She reached for Jessica's hand and held it tightly.

The light swept across the floor once, twice, three times. Elizabeth tried to stop thinking, just in case the man could hear that too. She watched with panicked eyes as the beam slid across the walls and the corners of the room.

There was silence.

"Rats, I guess," the man said at last. The flashlight beam bobbed up and down and suddenly appeared on the door of the gallery. "Better tell Charlie to get those exterminators back." Slowly the footsteps receded. After a moment the room was dark again, dark and silent as a tomb.

Elizabeth shakily got to her feet. "That was a close call," she whispered.

"You said it." Jessica's palm was soaked with sweat. "Let's get out of here!"

Together they crept to the entrance of the building. Checking to see that no one was watching, they dashed through the door and all the way back to Woodbridge Hall.

Safe. Safe at last.

But Elizabeth suspected she'd be seeing that ugly face in her dreams for a while longer.

Eleven

◇

"Hey, Jessica!" Bernard said when she arrived for ceramics class the next morning. "Hear the news?"

"What news?" Grinning at Bernard, Jessica draped her jacket over the back of her chair. With any luck, he'd drop another poem in her pocket today.

"About the gallery," Bernard said. He leaned against a cart loaded with pottery. "Someone snuck in last night!"

Jessica gulped. "Did they really?" She hoped that no one would pin it on her. What if they used bloodhounds to track her down? What if the bloodhounds were right now outside the door of the ceramics class? She sniffed her shoulder, hoping she didn't have much of a smell.

"Yeah," Bernard said, shaking his head. "I mean,

can you believe it? Sneaking into a little gallery like this, in the middle of the night? Like, hello?"

"That's—that's awful," Jessica agreed. "Whoever it was ought to be, you know, shot."

"At *least*." Bernard snorted. "One of the security guys heard a noise, but he thought it was rats."

"Oh." Jessica's mind raced. "Then—um—how did he know they were there?" *I didn't leave a shoe behind or anything, did I?* No, she was pretty sure she hadn't.

"Because of the pot." Bernard pushed gently on the cart. "It was stolen."

"Pot?" Jessica stared curiously at Bernard. "What pot?"

"The curse pot." Bernard shrugged. "You know about it, right? In the back corner of the gallery, on that high shelf. Sure, you've seen it," he went on as Jessica began to make strangled noises. "You, like, based your own pot on it, right?"

Jessica swallowed hard. "It—the curse pot can't be gone!"

"Can't be?" Bernard's eyes opened wide. "What do you mean, Jessica? It *is*."

"But it *can't* be," Jessica went on doggedly. She shut her eyes, trying to figure out how to explain this. "Because—last night—when we were—" She caught herself just in time. The curse pot had to be there, because she herself had been one of the intruders. And because she hadn't taken it with her. No way, José.

But of course she couldn't explain how she knew.

Bernard leaned closer. "Look, kid, the pot is history. Trust me on this. I saw the empty space this morning. I was, like, the guy who called in the alarm, OK?" He stretched out his arms like an umpire signaling safe. "It's *gone*."

"If you say so," Jessica mumbled. "Was anything else taken?"

Bernard laughed. "I wish! There's some real junk back there, but did the thief take that? No sirree. And you'd think a robber would take the really valuable stuff, but not *this* robber. No, they just took the one thing."

Jessica bit her lip. So the pot had disappeared. And nothing else. It couldn't be just a coincidence that the pot disappeared right after Susan had vanished, could it? Obviously it had to do with Susan.

And who would know the connection? The old woman, that was who. Jessica *had* to find the old woman. She had to be the one who held the key to the puzzle.

"Hello?" Bernard waved his hand in front of Jessica's face. "Anybody home?"

"Listen, Bernard." Jessica's mouth felt dry. "There's this old lady who sometimes comes to the galleries." Quickly she described the woman to him. "I—I only saw her once, so she might, you know, look different other times," she said hurriedly, "but it's, like, really important that I find her as quickly as possible. Do you know her?"

"Sure." Bernard shrugged. "I've seen her lots of times. She's a local artist, does some pretty outrageous stuff. What do you want with her anyway?"

Jessica decided not to tell him the truth. "I found something of hers," she lied, "and I wanted to return it. And maybe have a talk with her about art. Do you know her name and where she lives?"

"Her name's Hatta," Bernard said slowly, staring up at the fluorescent lights on the ceiling. "Yeah, Hatta. Hatta—McMurlow, McMorton, something like that. And she lives out on a river near here. That's where she gets the clay for her work," he told her. "See, there's, like, five hundred zillion years' worth of glacial deposits in the flood plain, and she scoops it up and it's like no clay you ever felt before, and—"

Jessica, frankly, wasn't interested. "But where on the river?" she pressed.

Bernard scratched his head. "This is pretty important to you, huh?"

"Um—yeah," Jessica agreed dryly. *You could say that.*

"OK." Bernard nodded. "I've got some work to do while you're in class, but I'll ask around, get some info for you. On one condition."

Jessica hoped he didn't want to come along, but if that was it she'd just have to trust him and deal with it. "Name it," she said.

Bernard cracked a smile. "That you have lunch with me again today."

Jessica blushed despite herself. "You got it."

*   *   *

"Ethan?" Bravely, Elizabeth approached her teacher's desk after class was over. "I, um, wanted to apologize for last night?"

It was kind of awkward, apologizing for herself when she wasn't even the one who had caused the problem. It wasn't her fault, after all, that Jessica didn't know Romantic poetry from a hole in the ground. "I'm sorry I was so dithery and I hope I didn't ruin your evening with Geraldine."

Ethan smiled. "I understand. Sometimes I get a little dithery myself."

"Oh," Elizabeth said. She didn't think of Ethan as the dithery type, but perhaps he was. "I'm glad. I—I know Geraldine speaks very highly of you."

"Well, I think she's quite nice," Ethan said, running his hand through his hair. "I certainly enjoyed her company, and I thought her poetry was very lovely. Yours too," he added. "I did like 'Ode to a Rabbit.' And I, um, hope you liked mine."

"Yours?" Elizabeth frowned. She thought back. When had he told her about his own poetry? At the snack bar once, but that was when he thought she was Geraldine. She'd certainly never seen any of his poetry. Not that she could remember anyway.

"Oh surely you know what I'm talking about!" Ethan seemed embarrassed. "'Ode to Blue-Green . . .' Well, never mind." He grinned at her crookedly. "Anyway, I'm glad you stopped by. I have a message for Geraldine, but I don't have her phone number anywhere. Maybe you'll take it to her?"

Elizabeth nodded. "I see Geraldine most days. If you need to get hold of her, you can call her, I mean me, at my number here on campus and I'll tell her." She gave him the number, wondering what poem Ethan was talking about. "Ode to Blue Something or Other." It sounded familiar, but she couldn't quite place it. Wasn't there a song called "Blue Suede Shoes" or something? "What message should I take?"

Ethan smiled. "There's a concert tonight, and I have tickets."

"Oh." Elizabeth drew in her breath. "I'm sure Geraldine would love to go." A grin spread across her face. "I'll tell her as soon as I see her and—"

"Wait." Ethan held up his hand. "Here's the deal. I have three tickets. And I really, really want you to come with us."

"Me?" Elizabeth moistened her lips. *Uh-oh.* "I'd love to, Ethan," she said with a nervous giggle, "but I'm afraid I can't. You see—" She hesitated.

"Family problems?" Ethan asked glumly.

"Well, no. I mean, yes," Elizabeth babbled. "It's, like, complicated . . . wouldn't you rather take just her anyway? I know she can go, but I—just can't."

Ethan shook his head vigorously. "That—that won't do. It's, like, complicated."

Elizabeth frowned slightly. Was she being teased? "I—I really can't," she protested weakly.

"Sure you can. I insist." Ethan leaned back

against the chalkboard, arms folded. "In fact, if you don't come, you might as well tell Geraldine to forget it too. I'll cash in the concert tickets and go off to Tahiti to write poetry and die a melancholy death. 'Now more than ever seems it rich to die,'" he quoted, "'to cease upon the midnight with no pain.' Keats, 'Ode to a Nightingale.' So either you come, or I go die a Romantic death, OK?"

Elizabeth was pretty sure he was kidding. But if she wanted to bag Ethan as Geraldine, it was obvious she'd have to provide an Elizabeth too.

She was going to owe Jessica big time. Big, big time.

"Sure," she said, heaving a deep sigh. "I guess maybe I can make it after all."

"Elizabeth! I need you. Now!"

Jessica stood in Elizabeth's doorway, breathing hard. She'd left her lunch with Bernard early, still worried about Susan and the curse pot. "We have to go see a woman named, um—" She consulted the paper in her hand. "Named Hatta McMurtry, and she lives five miles outside town, and there's a bus that leaves in, like, ten minutes, so let's roll!"

"We have to?" Elizabeth took her eyes off the book on her desk. "Jessica, I have another essay to write."

"Write it later." Jessica had checked the bus

schedule already. There wasn't time to get into an argument. "We have to go now."

"Hatta McMurtry?" Marion frowned. "This isn't that same old lady you were telling us about last night, is it, Jessica?"

"Yup." Jessica's stomach was tying itself in knots. It was critical to get to Hatta's place as soon as possible. "But there's more," she said quickly. "Somebody else was in the gallery last night and took the curse pot, the original, I mean!"

"And you think it's supernatural." Marion's eyes bore deeply into Jessica's.

"Well, of course! Something weird's going on," Jessica said, "and we have to talk to Hatta and find out what it is. Before it's too late."

Marion sat back, a satisfied smile on her face. "You're wrong," she said. "Bet you anything. There's a perfectly reasonable explanation for Susan vanishing. And for the curse pot disappearing. And I'm going to find out what it is." She turned to Elizabeth. "Think they'll give me extra credit?"

Jessica chose to ignore Marion. "Please, Lizzie. *Please.* I—I can't do this all by myself."

Elizabeth frowned. "On one condition," she said, standing up.

Jessica was getting tired of conditions, but what choice did she have? "Name it," she said tiredly.

"That you be me again tonight," Elizabeth said

quickly. "And on the bus ride over, I'll pump you full of Romantic poetry so you won't come across like a total birdbrain again. Deal?"

Jessica sighed. Her sister was becoming crazier by the minute, but who was she to complain when there was an evil curse pot on the loose? "Deal!" she agreed.

Twelve

"This is truly the middle of nowhere," Jessica said, tightening her jaw. "I sure hope this is the right bus."

She pressed her nose against the window, watching the scenery roll by. The road had gone sharply up a mountain and then begun curving gently down the other side. Sheep grazed in a pasture of brownish grass on the left, and on the right a rocky cliff rose suddenly out of the ground. Everything looked dry and windswept, not at all like the rest of Sweet Valley.

"We could ask the driver again, I guess," Elizabeth murmured.

Jessica shook her head. She'd already asked him twice. *Come on,* she urged the bus driver silently. *Put the pedal to the metal and . . .*

In the distance a ribbon of silver appeared. She crossed her fingers. *Maybe that's the river Bernard was talking about.* Bernard had definitely told her that Hatta lived by a river. Something about clay.

Elizabeth poked her in the side. "What if Hatta's not home?" she hissed.

"She'll be home." Jessica tried to sound confident. Yes, it was definitely a river coming up to meet them. And off to the left, wasn't that a house? Jessica was almost sure that it was.

"But what if—" Elizabeth persisted.

"Zip your lip." Jessica felt huge butterflies flying around her stomach. Unless they were eagles. The bus rumbled across the river on a bumpy, narrow bridge with concrete embankments and pulled off the road.

"Here's your stop." The driver gestured to the girls and yanked open the door.

"Um—thanks." *I think.* Jessica led the way off the bus. Behind the twins, the door slid silently shut and the bus roared off.

Hatta's house—if it was Hatta's—looked a little creepy, Jessica thought. The roof tiles were a crazy quilt of colors. The front door was a luminous black, and the only window was a huge circular one right next to the road. A low stone wall surrounded the property. Strange-looking planters sat on the wall. Planters with huge ungainly flowers growing in them like weeds. Planters that were—wait a minute—

Sinks. Jessica started in surprise. The planters were definitely kitchen sinks. Except for one which was—

Jessica blinked.

"That's a toilet," Elizabeth said, rubbing her eyes. "She's planted marigolds in an old toilet!"

Jessica wiped her forehead. Obviously this lady was, like, totally bonkers. She turned back to the road, half hoping that the bus would be there again. Susan suddenly seemed a lot less important now. Like Marion said—there had to be a rational explanation. One thing was for sure, though: Jessica didn't want to go into a house where they grew marigolds in toilets and—

"Why, hello there! Won't you come in?" Hatta asked, throwing open the window and smiling out into the afternoon sunshine.

"Tea?" Hatta asked. She didn't wait for an answer, but poured tea from a kettle into three small ceramic cups, each glazed a different brilliant color. At least, Elizabeth assumed it was tea, though the thought crossed her mind that it might possibly be poison. "And I've got little tiny cucumber sandwiches and lacy cookies too!"

Jessica wrinkled her nose in a gesture that reminded Elizabeth a lot of Geraldine. Elizabeth had to agree that the cookies and sandwiches didn't look very appetizing.

"Come to the dining room," Hatta said to the

twins. "We'll sit and talk. How nice of you to come all this way just to see me!"

"Um—yeah," Jessica said. "You see, Ms. McMurtry—"

"Call me Hatta," the old woman suggested. "Everyone does." She opened a door and motioned the twins ahead of her. "My dining room doubles as a studio," she said apologetically. "You see, with only one of me I don't bother with the rules, and anyhow, I spend most of my time at work. I take only very short breaks. Often I don't leave the room for hours at a time."

Elizabeth felt she should say something. "Doesn't that get tiring?" she ventured.

The old woman laughed. "It's just like what my old friend Pablo Picasso used to say. 'Don't you get tired?' his friends would ask, and he'd reply, 'Dear, dear, no, I leave my body outside.'" She chuckled and set the tea tray down on a worktable. "I, too, leave my body outside when I work."

Elizabeth nodded, though she only half understood. "You've done some interesting stuff," she said, staring around the room. Every imaginable space was filled with pottery of one kind or another: birds in flight, brightly decorated bowls, plates with brooding patterns of gray and brown etched into their sides.

Hatta's face brightened. "Oh thank you so much!" she said. "Do help yourselves to tea and snacks. We don't stand on ceremony here, that's my motto. No need to ask; have a cucumber sand-wich." She passed Elizabeth the plate. "Take two, they're small, and anyway, they won't keep."

Elizabeth decided to take just one. She bit into it delicately and made a face. The bread was slightly stale, the cucumber a week or two past its peak, and the mayonnaise was spread way too thickly. She quickly passed the plate to Jessica. Maybe the lacy cookies would be better.

"I have teas for the university students every Tuesday and Wednesday at four," Hatta said, her eyes sparkling. "It's about all I do besides work. And visiting the gallery, of course."

Gag! The lacy cookies weren't much better after all.

"That's actually what we wanted to talk to you about, Hatta," Jessica said, beginning to choke on a cu-cumber sandwich. "The gallery. There was this pot . . . a curse pot, I guess, that you showed me. And it's—"

"You mean this one?" Hatta beamed and reached behind her. From a low shelf she pulled out a pot and held it out for inspection.

Elizabeth gasped. There was no doubt about it. The pot was the curse pot.

"That one," Jessica wheezed. Her eyes were bulging. "Where—how—"

"I took it, of course." Hatta looked from Elizabeth to Jessica and back. "Well, of course I took it! It's my pot, after all. I made it. Or didn't you know that?"

"N-No," Elizabeth said slowly.

"I—I *didn't* know that," Jessica said, her breathing returning to normal. She passed the snack plate back to Elizabeth. "You didn't *tell* me."

Hatta laughed lightly. "Yes, I lent it to the gallery. And I wanted it back. So I took it. Did I forget to leave a note? Too careless of me!" She frowned at the plate in Elizabeth's hands. "Now don't stand on ceremony, my dears. Have more cucumber sandwiches. They're extremely tasty today!"

Elizabeth gave a faint nod and passed the plate again. "But—how did you do it?" she asked.

"Did you turn yourself into a—a black cat?" Jessica asked, her voice quivery with fright. "Or—or fly through the walls?"

Hatta chuckled and reached into her pocket. "Nothing that elaborate. Have you ever seen one of these?"

A key? Elizabeth blinked. "You just unlocked the door?"

"Naturally." Hatta sipped her tea thoughtfully. "Years ago, I taught a class or two at the college. The key still fits."

Jessica frowned and passed the plate of snacks back to Elizabeth, not having taken any more. "But why?"

The smile left Hatta's face. "I had a feeling about that curse pot. I'm a highly intuitive person, you understand, and when I get feelings I take them seriously. I felt that it might be giving young people the wrong idea about art." She leaned forward. "Art must be a force for good. Never for ill will."

"I understand." Elizabeth bit her lip. Even though she didn't exactly believe Jessica's story about cursing Susan, she could relate to what Hatta was saying.

"But—" Jessica swallowed hard. "I—I *did* get an idea. From your pot, I mean." Her eyes were avoiding Hatta's face. "I—I created my own curse pot. With my roommate's face. And now—she's disappeared." Her body sagged against the table.

Hatta paused with her teacup halfway to her lips. "Oh, dear," she said gravely.

Elizabeth's heart was beating fast. "A curse pot's not *real*, it's just for fun," she argued. But still, there was something in Hatta's eyes that made her less sure than she wanted to be.

"Is there any way to reverse the curse?" Jessica's eyes were pleading.

"A reversal—I don't know." Hatta looked thoughtfully into space. "I will think about it," she promised. "If I come up with anything, I shall not hesitate to get in touch with you." Then the smile returned to her face. "Eat up!" she said heartily. "Have some more cucumber sandwiches! Remember, we don't stand on ceremony here!"

"Well, I don't care," Jessica insisted. She sat cross-legged on Elizabeth's bed, still thinking about the curse pot at Hatta's house. "Even if she did get the pot in a normal way, I still think something weird's happened to Susan." In fact, though she didn't want to admit it to Elizabeth and Marion, she was a little afraid to go into her own room, afraid of the curse pot she'd made with the horrible picture of Susan scratched into its side.

"She probably just left," Elizabeth said. "She up and went home."

"Then why is her stuff still in the room?" Jessica demanded.

Elizabeth rubbed the side of her nose. "Maybe there was a family emergency. Maybe she, like, got so homesick she couldn't stand it."

"I've been doing some sleuthing," Marion said darkly. "She may have been last seen in the company of a guy named Mike. Remember him? He was at our table for a little while at the snack bar that first night. Till Susan dragged him away."

Jessica remembered, all right. "So what are you saying?" she asked.

Marion narrowed her eyes. "Well, murder's always a possibility."

Of course, murder could be connected with the curse pot too. Jessica shuddered, seeing the two pots in her mind's eye. Susan strangled, at the bottom of a high cliff . . . Susan pushed down a flight of stairs by Mike, the homicidal maniac . . . If only she'd never noticed the first pot to begin with, maybe all this wouldn't have happened. "But . . . didn't you think there was something weird about Hatta?" she asked Elizabeth.

"You mean besides the cucumber sandwiches?" Elizabeth tossed her head. "No, Jess. Marion's right. It felt kind of weird there for a while, but that was just the house. She's a harmless old lady, a little lonely is all." She smiled. "And now that we're back here where things are familiar, it's obvious that there's a reasonable explanation."

Jessica shook her head. "You guys are so wrong," she muttered. Why did she have this feeling of impending doom?

"Anyway, Jess," Elizabeth said, "we have to get ready for our big date tonight. Remember what I taught you on the bus? Quick, who was Lord Byron?"

"Lord Byron?" Jessica sighed. She'd forgotten about having to play Elizabeth. "He was, like, one of the founders of the Romantics."

"Very good." Elizabeth nodded, pleased. "Complete these lines: 'Tyger, tyger, burning bright . . .'"

"'In the forests of the night?'" Jessica strained to think. *Or was it 'shadows?'* "In the something of the night." That way you could leave it to the reader's imagination.

Elizabeth rolled her eyes just as the phone rang. Quickly she scooped up the receiver. "Hello," she said breathlessly. "Elizabeth Wakefield speaking."

"Who is it?" Jessica smiled, glad to be off the hook about shadows and forests.

"Oh—hi, Ethan." Elizabeth turned her back to Jessica.

"Major crush," Marion observed with a sigh. "So you're going to be Elizabeth, huh? The mind reels." She reached for her disguises book. "Want a little help from an expert? You're going to need to know *way* more than a few poems to pass."

"You *what*?" Elizabeth said into the phone. There was disbelief in her voice. "*Four* of them? Because you're a faculty member?"

Four what? Jessica leaned closer. Marion did too.

"But—but Ethan—" Elizabeth clamped the receiver to her ear. "I—I can't just do that. What if she has plans of her own?" She listened intently. "But couldn't you, like, give away the extra ticket?"

Jessica sighed. She had the feeling that Elizabeth had things backward. Maybe Jessica should have played glamorous old Geraldine while Elizabeth played herself. Geraldine didn't need to know all about the Romantic poets anyway. Plus, Jessica knew way more about fashion than . . . "No, it isn't family problems," Elizabeth said.

"What's she talking about?" Marion mouthed to Jessica, but Jessica could only shrug.

"OK," Elizabeth said slowly. Jessica thought her eyes looked a little frantic. "She's here. Let me ask her." Holding her hand over the mouthpiece, she called across the room. "Oh *Jessica!* You're not doing anything tonight, are you? How'd you like to attend a really cool concert with Geraldine and her boyfriend and me?"

Now how are we going to manage that, Lizzie? Jessica thought irritably. *Since I'm going as you and you're going as somebody who doesn't even exist . . .* What did Elizabeth expect her to do—be both twins at once? She could see herself now, dashing from one chair to the other so fast Ethan wouldn't notice, saying "Ah, what a lovely performance!" as Elizabeth and then saying "Yeah, but the drums weren't loud enough" as herself. And if Elizabeth thought *that* was going to net her a boyfriend, well, she had another thing coming—

"Why, I'd love to!" Marion exclaimed brightly.

Jessica blinked. So she was going as Elizabeth and Marion was going as . . . Jessica?

A look of relief crossed Elizabeth's face. Quickly she put the phone back to her ear. "Ethan?" she said into the receiver. "You're in luck. She'd be delighted!"

Thirteen

"Well, Jessica! Great to meet you," Ethan said with a grin. "I've heard a lot about you from your sisters here."

It took a lot of effort for Jessica, the real Jessica, not to answer. Fortunately, Marion remembered who she was supposed to be. "No problem," she gushed, pumping Ethan's hand. "I've been hearing so much about you from Geraldine and Elizabeth, I feel like you're already practically part of the family!"

Jessica snorted. She didn't sound like that! It was lucky, she reflected, that Marion looked so much like her and her sister. They'd done Marion's hair in a style similar to Jessica's—or was it Elizabeth's?—and Marion had practiced doing a Jessica imitation all afternoon. They could probably pass for fraternal twins anyway.

"Hi, Elizabeth." Ethan turned to Jessica and winked. "Nice to, um, see you again."

"Hi, Ethan," Jessica said shyly, trying to imitate her sister. "Wasn't it a shame about poor John Keats? I've been brooding about him all afternoon," she went on sadly. "Such a great poet . . . and dying when he was less than thirty . . ." She might as well make use of all the knowledge that her sister had drummed into her.

Elizabeth, or rather Geraldine, coughed disapprovingly. "Well, it's so nice to see you, Ethan!" she said sweetly, grasping his elbow.

"What a shame about Keats," Ethan agreed. He kept looking straight at Jessica. Apparently he was in no hurry to greet Geraldine.

"No telling how many poems he would have written if he'd lived to be, like, a hundred and six," Jessica said brightly, wishing that Ethan would quit staring at her.

"That's not the point, Elizabeth, and you know it," Elizabeth huffed. "The whole deal with Keats is that his suffering helped him create such great literature. Isn't that right, Ethan?" Her fingers worked their way down to his hand.

"Who wants to suffer?" Marion grimaced. "Give me a nice life and I'll quit being creative forever."

Ethan's eyes didn't leave Jessica's face. "Well, Elizabeth has a good point, Geraldine," he said. "We don't know what Keats might have written if he'd lived and hadn't suffered so much. Maybe it would have been terrible. Maybe wonderful. Who knows what makes a genius? But enough of this—let's go find our seats." He stepped toward the auditorium entrance. The three girls followed.

"I don't get it," Jessica mumbled to Marion. "Why did he care so much about having you come—I mean, having me come?"

"Beats me." Marion shrugged. "Who are you anyway? I forgot."

Jessica sighed. She trailed along after Ethan as he headed down the aisle. *You are Elizabeth,* she reminded herself. *You are Elizabeth Wakefield, and if somebody calls you "Jessica" you smile and say, "Oh you must mean my sister," and point to Elizabeth—no, to Marion . . .* She sighed again.

If they could get through this OK, they'd all deserve a medal.

"Here we are!" Ethan said happily, arriving at their row. "Geraldine, you're on the inside, then me, then Elizabeth, and Jessica nearest the aisle."

"Sure," Jessica said, hanging back for the others to go first before she remembered that she was really Elizabeth.

"Always the last one," Marion whined, settling into her seat. There was an empty chair between her and the aisle. "Just because you guys come first in alphabetical order—"

"Now, now, Jessica," Ethan interrupted her. His eyes twinkled. "There's method to my madness, as Shakespeare said."

"Shakespeare, indeed," Elizabeth cooed in a most un-Elizabeth-like voice. "You'll study Shakespeare someday, girls. When you're a little older."

"So where do you go to school, Jessica?" Ethan asked.

Jessica jumped, but Marion answered. "Oh school," she said dismissively. "You know how school is." Her eyes, troubled, seemed to send messages to Jessica and Elizabeth. "School's—school!"

"I don't really know," Ethan said shyly. "I haven't told Geraldine or Elizabeth this, but—"

"She goes to Sweet Valley Middle School, right, Jessica?" Elizabeth said.

"Right," Jessica agreed, casting a puzzled glance at her sister. Too late she remembered that she was Elizabeth tonight—and that the real Elizabeth had answered because the real Marion wouldn't have known where the real Jessica went to school. Or something. She coughed and said, "Right, Jessica?"

"Sweet Valley Middle, yeah," Marion agreed. "But I'm not, like, studious the way these guys are. I mean, you could Shakespeare me all day long and I'd probably never notice." She shrugged. "Some people get all the good genes, what can I say?"

Jessica rolled her eyes. She did too know about Shakespeare. He'd written *Romeo and Juliet* and . . . and . . . and a bunch of other things, and his first name was William—well, William or Henry or George, one of those. She swallowed hard. "I think

Jessica's a lot smarter than that," she said in defense of somebody, she wasn't sure who anymore.

Ethan's eyes twinkled. He slid a little closer to her. "That's loyalty for you," he said. "Stick up for your sister, no matter what. One of your best traits, Elizabeth. 'Of loyal nature and of noble mind,'" he quoted, grinning. "Tennyson described you to a T."

"Um—thanks," Jessica said, wondering what he was talking about. She looked around. The auditorium was nearly full, though the seat by Marion was still empty. She wished the concert would hurry up and start. This was too hard.

Ethan raised his eyebrows. "Yet you are artistic, Jessica. Not in the realm of poetry, true. But if you add a T to poetry and rearrange the letters?" His lips parted in a shy smile and he stared at Marion.

"Um—," Marion said, making a face that looked surprisingly like Jessica's own. "Me, artistic?" she said with a disparaging laugh.

"Poetry plus a T equals pottery," Elizabeth whispered over Ethan's head, making frantic signs with her hands.

Aha! "He means my—your—ceramics," Jessica explained. "Tell him about the pot you made, OK?"

"The curse pot, right?" Ethan asked. "I heard about that—the face etched into the side and glazed in the kiln to perfection."

Jessica couldn't help smiling. It sounded like a recipe.

"Oh that old thing," Marion said, curling her lip.

"Well, I, like, took this clay, right? Then I tossed in some more clay and stuck it together with, um, even more clay, and made pictures in the side, and—" She shrugged. "I had a pot."

"It was a little harder than that," Jessica protested. She could feel Ethan's arm brush lightly against her back, where her jacket was hanging. "Didn't it take, like, hours and hours?" No way was she going to let anybody think she hadn't worked hard on that piece of art.

Marion grinned. "Whatever you say, Je—um, Elizabeth."

Jessica twisted uneasily in her seat, wondering how Ethan had known about her pottery. Had he had spies in the ceramics building? Elizabeth, the actual Elizabeth, might have told him in her persona as Geraldine, but it didn't seem likely that she would have told about the curse pot in any detail. But then how—

"So Elizabeth is generous of spirit too," Ethan observed, winking at Jessica.

"Excuse me, is this seat taken?" a familiar voice asked. "Hey, Eth!"

"Hey, Bernard! Fancy meeting you here!" Ethan replied, a cat-that-ate-the-canary grin on his face. "You know this guy or something?" he asked Marion, unable to keep the delight out of his voice.

"Um—" Marion looked helplessly at Jessica.

"Oh sure," Bernard said. He slid into the empty

seat and smiled across Marion to Jessica. "We've, um, run into each other before, huh?"

It's a setup, Jessica realized, staring from Bernard to Ethan and back. Obviously the two guys knew each other. Probably even were friends. She drew in her breath, remembering that Bernard had told her how he'd met a couple of really neat guys already . . .

They must have gotten to talking and realized that they were interested in sisters, she told herself. *Even though one of them was interested in a sister that didn't really exist.* Her mind whirled. Bernard and Ethan had planned this, that was clear. She saw it all now. Bernard and his "Is this seat taken?" Ethan and his "Fancy meeting you here!" *"Won't Jessica be surprised,"* they'd probably said.

And Jessica was surprised.

The only problem was, Jessica was actually Marion, who was completely clueless where Bernard was concerned, and the real Jessica was— Elizabeth.

"Delighted to meet you, Bernard," Elizabeth said in a strangled voice. "I'm, um, Geraldine." She flashed Jessica a terrified "now-what?" look, and Jessica knew that her sister was thinking exactly the same thing.

"Have you met Elizabeth?" Ethan clapped Jessica affectionately on the shoulder. "Elizabeth, this is Jessica's friend Bernard. My friend too."

"Get your eyes checked, Eth." Bernard laughed.

"That's not Elizabeth. That's Jessica, anybody knows that." He smiled at Jessica.

"N-no," Ethan said slowly, gesturing toward Marion. *"That one's Jessica."*

"Of course I'm Jessica," Marion said stoutly. "I was when I woke up this morning anyway." But nobody laughed.

"You've been reading too many poetry books, Ethan," Bernard scoffed.

Ethan frowned. "And I'm telling *you*, Bernard, you've been hanging around too many empty pots. *This* is the one I've been telling you about—the kid in the poetry class who's so brilliant." He nodded to Jessica. "Only she's *Elizabeth*."

Jessica looked frantically at the others. This wasn't going well. There was only one thing to do under the circumstances.

"Oooh!" she moaned, doubling up in sudden agony.

"Are you all right?" Bernard and Ethan leaned toward her simultaneously, concern clouding their faces.

"Nooo," Jessica gasped, lying through her teeth. "My stomach . . ." She breathed deeply. "Listen, I hate to disappoint you guys, but I have to go . . . lie down."

"Me too," Elizabeth moaned. "All of a sudden . . ."

"Oh yeah." Marion winced with pain. "Must have been something I ate. I feel like I'm about to barf!"

The girls rose unsteadily from their seats and staggered up the aisle just as the lights started to dim. "Good-bye, guys, and thanks for a pleasant time," Elizabeth called back.

"*That* was the disaster of the century," Elizabeth said sadly. She was draped across her bed, the "Geraldine" outfit askew, but she didn't even care. It still wasn't clear to her exactly what had happened. "So you knew that guy, Jessica?"

Jessica bobbed her head. "I know Bernard, all right. But what I didn't know was that he knew, um, your guy."

"And of course Jessica's guy knew that I wasn't Jessica," Marion added helpfully, "but Elizabeth's guy didn't know that, so he believed us when we said I was. So it was kind of confusing when the girl he thought was Elizabeth turned out to be the same girl his buddy thought was Jessica."

Elizabeth groaned and stretched out. "Now I'm afraid to face Ethan in class tomorrow. Especially if he and Bernard begin comparing notes."

"They'll certainly think the Wakefields are one of the great dysfunctional families of the planet," Marion observed. "Did you know that, like, eighty-five percent of all criminals come from dysfunctional families?"

Elizabeth was too unhappy to laugh. She could see it now. Ethan would say "But I'm sure that one was Elizabeth!" and Bernard would answer "No, I'm positive it's Jessica." And if they found out the truth . . .

Good-bye, crush, she thought bleakly.

"That's strange." Jessica spoke almost to herself. Elizabeth jerked her head up to see her twin staring down at a note in her hands—a piece of creamy white paper folded neatly into fourths. "He must have written me another one," she murmured, opening it, "only he wasn't sitting next to me—and we left right when he came in . . ."

"What are you talking about?" Elizabeth wanted to know.

"Oh Bernard's been writing me poems." Jessica unfolded the sheet and nodded. "Yup, it's from him, all right. Same handwriting, same ink, everything."

"Poems?" Elizabeth frowned. "Let me see?" she asked.

"Well—it's kind of private." But Jessica graciously handed her the sheet.

"'On First Gazing into Her Kindly Face,'" Elizabeth read. Furrowing her brow, she read the first stanza softly aloud:

Ah, sweet vale of knowledge! How oft have
I strayed,
All weary with love, down thy pathways
and bowers?
'Tis truly a college which learning hath made.
Yet never learned I of the scent of the flowers—
Nor the green of the thickets, the birds in
their place,

Till that night on the bridge when I first saw
her face.

"Pretty cool, huh?" Jessica was turning faintly
pink. "I'm kind of surprised Bernard's such a, you
know, a good poet. Not that I'm complaining or
anything. Of course," she added, "he made a few
things up. We didn't meet on a bridge. We met
when I ran into his cart outside the ceramics room."

Elizabeth's mouth felt dry. She stared at the first
stanza of the poem again. "Um—Jess," she said,
faltering. "I was the one who met him on a bridge."

"You met Bernard on a bridge?" Jessica asked
doubtfully.

"No, not Bernard." Elizabeth closed her eyes.
Something—something Ethan had said earlier, and
something Jessica had said too . . . "Um—you said
he wrote you another poem too?"

"Uh-huh." Jessica blinked rapidly. "'Ode to
Blue-Green Eyes,' it was called. I'm so glad he noticed them. Lila always says they're not my best
feature, but she's just jealous. The poem's in my
room somewhere."

"'Ode to Blue-Green Eyes.'" Elizabeth bit her
lip. *This isn't making any sense.* "Listen . . . Bernard
didn't write these poems. Ethan did."

"Get out!" Jessica snorted. "How could he? He
doesn't even know me!"

Elizabeth folded her arms. She didn't know
what to think, but one thing was for sure. "Ethan

wrote them. If you guys have been hanging around together . . . well, that's OK, I guess, but tell me at least." *A real Romantic heroine would cry and scream and carry on,* she thought, a lump in her throat. *And refuse to ever look at another guy again. I guess I'm just not a proper Romantic heroine . . .*

"We can check this out easily," Marion said. "Elizabeth, where's that essay you wrote the other day—the one with the *A*-plus-plus on it?"

Mechanically Elizabeth opened the desk drawer and gave Marion the essay. Marion spread it out on the bed next to the poem. "Well, it doesn't take my parents to see this one. Elizabeth, you're right. Look."

The twins crowded around as Marion explained. "Notice the way he makes his *H*s, with that extra little point on top. And the way the *Y*s come way down under all the other letters? Then there's the crossed *T*s—" She pointed them out. "And the dots on the *I*s are always a little to the right of the stem of the letter."

"It's the same writing," Jessica agreed. "But why would Ethan have dropped it into my pocket?"

"Because he has a crush on you," Elizabeth said sadly. He must have put the poem in the pocket when they were in the auditorium, she decided. Now that she thought about it, she'd seen Ethan's arm snaking over behind Jessica and—

"No, dummy." Marion sighed heavily. "He has a crush on *you*."

"On *me*?" Elizabeth touched her chest, surprised.

"On which me? On me me or on Jessica me?"

"On the real Elizabeth, duh," Marion answered. "The one in his poetry class who made so many insightful comments."

"But . . ." Elizabeth shook her head. She didn't get it at all.

"Is it always so hard with you two around?" Marion asked wryly. "You really need a keen analytical mind such as my own. Look. It's obvious. He notices this kid in his class who loves poetry, OK?"

"OK," Elizabeth agreed hesitantly.

"And where did he meet this kid? On a bridge, right? Here at SVU—a 'college which learning hath made.'" Marion tapped the poem impatiently. "I'm, like, the world's worst poetry person, and even I got that part. So he talks up this kid, because he thinks she's, like, way cool, only she's too dense to see it."

"I am not either too dense to—," Elizabeth began.

"Sure you are," Marion interrupted, grinning at Elizabeth. "You're book smart, but you're not smart smart, like me. Anyway, this kid doesn't get it. She thinks he could never go for her because she's too young, so she invents an older sister and becomes that sister, am I right so far?"

Elizabeth made a face. "So far," she agreed.

"But the guy isn't interested in the older sister," Marion went on. "He's interested in the younger one. Only the younger one keeps turning down dates and lunches and stuff, so he starts writing her poems to show how he feels."

A suspicion was growing in Elizabeth. "So the poems were for me. Go on," she prompted.

"Plus," Marion said, "the sister keeps dressing up as the older one and showing off her twin as herself. So guess what happens when he wants to give her the poem without her knowing it?"

Jessica hit herself on the side of the head. "The cafeteria," she groaned. "I should have guessed. He must have—"

"He probably dropped that first poem in your pocket in the crowded cafeteria," Marion added. "Thinking you were Elizabeth. So he's got a crush on you—" She pointed to Elizabeth. "Only he thinks she's you." She pointed dramatically to Jessica.

"Oh," Elizabeth said weakly. Her mind flashed back to that evening in the snack bar when Jessica had come barging in. She'd mentioned an ode that someone had given her. What had Ethan said? *"It wasn't about eyes, by any chance?"* And then the next day in class . . . when Ethan had made that cryptic comment about how he hoped she'd liked his poetry. . . .

It all fit. She reached for the poem and scanned the first stanza again. "Till that night on the bridge when I first saw her face," she read.

"He does like me after all," she murmured, thinking back to that night.

And for the first time in quite a while, Elizabeth broke into a smile.

Fourteen

"Elizabeth?"

Ethan ran his hand through his hair in that familiar gesture. "I don't know how to tell you this, exactly," he said shyly, "but I guess I need to. It's about Geraldine."

"Yes?" Friday's class had just ended, and Elizabeth was slowly gathering up books. She'd wondered if Ethan would approach her first, or if she'd have to speak up instead. "About, um, yesterday evening . . . we're all really sorry we, um, got sick so suddenly, and I hope you guys enjoyed the concert."

"To tell you the truth, I didn't stay. I was there for one reason only, and it wasn't the concert. No." Ethan shook his head. "Listen, Elizabeth. I know Geraldine likes me and all, but . . . she's too old for me."

"Too—old?" Elizabeth squeaked. This made no sense. How could an eighteen-year-old be too old for a college student? "I mean—"

Abruptly she broke off. She'd come to class ready to say that "Geraldine" wasn't that interested in him after all. *Cool your jets and let him finish*, she told herself sternly.

Ethan smiled his toothy grin. "To tell the truth, I've just turned sixteen myself," he confided. "I was . . . kind of a genius, and they kept passing me through the grades. As I look back, I'd have been better off with kids my own age instead of skipping all the time, but . . ." He shrugged. "I don't advertise it exactly, but I'm younger than you think."

"Oh." Elizabeth blinked. So Ethan was only four years older than she was. Less, even, if he'd just had a birthday. She drew in her breath. "OK, Ethan," she said happily. "No problem. I'll, like, explain things to her."

Ethan nodded soberly. "I don't want to hurt her feelings or anything."

"Don't worry," Elizabeth assured him. "I know Geraldine pretty well, and I have a feeling she'll be OK."

"There's something else too." Ethan leaned against the chalkboard, getting chalk dust all over his blue sweater. "The one I was interested in all the time was, well, not to put too fine a point on it, um—you. And I hope my poems weren't too embarrassing for you to read," he added quickly, staring at the floor. "It's just that . . . that words are how I express myself, and, um, I guess you know by now how much I love Romantic poetry, so . . ." He swallowed hard. "You can tear them up if you'd like."

"Oh no!" Elizabeth stared at Ethan in horror. "I'd never do a thing like that!" she protested. "I'm going to keep them in a scrapbook and save them forever."

A shy smile flickered across Ethan's face. "Then you—didn't mind. I didn't really know. Sometimes it was kind of hard to tell with you."

You don't know the half of it, Elizabeth thought. "As a matter of fact, I liked them so much I wrote you one of my own," she said, digging in her backpack for the verse she'd spent all last evening on.

"Really?" Ethan stood up straighter and beamed.

"Really," Elizabeth told him. Feeling more than a little nervous, she handed him "Lines Inscribed to a Newfound Friend."

"I think you'll find it's a little more sophisticated than, um, 'Ode to a Rabbit,'" she said wryly.

"I'm sorry about last night, Bernard," Jessica said shyly. It was after ceramics class, and she was standing in the hall. "I, um, wasn't exactly myself."

"Oh that's OK," Bernard said, grinning. "Are you all right? I was kind of worried when you guys just got up and left."

"Just fine," Jessica said. She'd been nervous about approaching Bernard, but it seemed like he was taking it OK. "Um—how was the concert?" she ventured.

"It rocked," Bernard said happily. "Ol' Ethan left the moment you guys did, practically, but not me." He winked at Jessica. "Sometime we'll have to go hear one together for real."

"Yeah," Jessica agreed. She couldn't help but smile. "Listen, um, Bernard, there's something I wanted to tell you." Quickly she explained about the curse pot she'd made and how it had spirited Susan away. "I'm a little embarrassed to be asking you," she said faintly, "but I thought—since you're such an artist—maybe you had some ideas?"

Bernard made a face. "So that's why you wanted to go see Hatta What's-her-name," he said thoughtfully.

Jessica nodded. "McMurtry. Yeah, we went there, and I asked her. But she said she didn't know if you could, like, undo a curse."

"Hmm." Bernard stroked his chin. "She probably said she'd think about it, am I right? She's always saying that."

"That's right," Jessica admitted. "Maybe we should call her to see if she's come up with anything."

Bernard shook his head. "Hatta doesn't have a phone. She says it's just one of those 'modern contrivances' she can do without."

"Oh." Jessica bit her lip. She couldn't imagine living without a phone, personally, but Hatta was definitely not a normal sort of person. "Then—I guess—that's that."

"Oh come on." Bernard smiled. "There's a bus, isn't there? Let's go visit her. You can bring your curse pot. And I've always wanted to go see her house. I hear the teas she gives students on Tuesdays and Wednesdays are awesome."

"You could say that," Jessica agreed, slipping her arm casually into Bernard's. "If you like stale cucumber sandwiches!"

"This is truly fine workmanship," Hatta said slowly, turning Jessica's pot around and around in her hands. Her eyes sparkled brightly.

"Thank you," Jessica said, feeling proud despite herself.

"The pot has flaws." Hatta peered over the tops of her spectacles at Jessica. "And a curse pot must always have flaws. It ought never to be perfect."

"No one ever accused my sister of being perfect," Elizabeth said, sending the snack plate on to Bernard. Jessica had run into Elizabeth and Ethan on their way to the bus stop and gotten them to come along. Now they were all four busily not eating cucumber sandwiches and lacy cookies.

"Oh eat, eat, eat," Hatta directed Bernard, beaming broadly. "We don't stand on ceremony here! Girls are always on diets and never eat many of the snacks I prepare, but it's different for boys, isn't it? Don't stint yourself. You need meat on your bones."

Bernard shuddered and slipped three lacy cookies off the plate. "Here, Ethan, have some cucumber sandwiches," Bernard said meaningfully, passing the plate on.

"Gee, um, thanks," Ethan said with a cough.

"And the flowing lines of the design." Gently, Hatta stroked the rim of the pot. "An outstanding job, my dear."

"Thanks," Jessica said again. "But—really—the reason I came to you was something else. Is there—" How could she say this in a way that wouldn't sound incredibly stupid? "Is there a way of freeing Susan from the evil spell?"

Hatta's eyes took on a downcast look. "I know of no easy way. The only possibility is—" She hesitated and stared, frowning, at Jessica's pot.

"What?" Jessica asked. She could feel her heart pounding in her chest.

"Interesting," Hatta said thoughtfully, fingering the pot. "I hadn't noticed before. Bernard, my boy, do you know where this clay came from?"

Bernard sat up straight, avoiding Ethan's efforts to pass the snack plate back to him. "Well—," he said, frowning. "It looks familiar, but I can't place it. One thing's for certain. It's not the kind the department usually buys."

"Correct," Hatta said, smiling at Bernard as if he

were her prize pupil. "Once in a while I donate some of my special riverbank clay to the college. During flood season there's so much more than I can use—well, you don't care about that. At any rate, Jessica, you've used clay from right here to make your curse pot."

"OK," Jessica said uncertainly. "So, um, now that we know that, what do we do?" She wished Hatta would get to the point.

"Some say that the curse can be destroyed if the pot is destroyed and returned to the place from which it came," Hatta said slowly, her eyes seeming far away. "I cannot tell for certain whether the tale is true, but perhaps it is worth a try. Do you understand what I am saying, my dear?"

"I—I think so." Jessica nodded. "If the pot gets shattered, then maybe the spirit will be released." She frowned, concentrating intently.

"And if the pieces of the pot go back to their home," Elizabeth said slowly, "then the spirit will too. Go back to its home, I mean. That makes sense."

"'Break, break, break,'" Ethan quoted in a mournful voice, "'on the cold gray stones, O pot!'" He grinned. "Tennyson. Sort of."

"I knew that," Jessica said crossly. She held out her arms for the pot.

"Well?" she asked the others. "What are you waiting for?"

*   *   *

"I sure hope this works," Jessica said dubiously. She stood on the riverbank holding the pot in front of her while Elizabeth and the two boys watched.

"It's a beautiful place, anyway," Elizabeth said, looking up and down the river. To the right the water rolled on down to the ocean, muddy and slow. To the left the stream was narrower and clearer and ran across low rocks on its way from the mountains. The bridge blocked her view after a few yards, but in the distance she could make out a shimmering band where the river met the horizon. "It's just—such a shame to wreck the pot, Jess. Are you sure . . ." Her voice trailed off.

"It was a beauty, all right," Bernard agreed. He stood with his hands jammed into his pockets. "I wish—well . . ."

"'Beauty is truth, truth beauty,'" Ethan quoted solemnly. "'That is all ye know on earth, and all ye need to know.' Keats."

Elizabeth swallowed hard. She thought she understood what Ethan meant. The true beauty of the pot would only be revealed if it brought Susan back.

If she believed that the pot had made her disappear to begin with, of course.

Which she didn't, not really . . .

"I think you'll have to smash it, Jess," she said. "You could always make another one if you wanted."

"Never again," Jessica said grimly. "I will never

make another curse pot again in my entire life. Not if I live to be three million and two." She lifted the pot above her head. "Here goes nothing."

"Shouldn't there be, like, some kind of ceremony first?" Bernard asked. "Poetry readings and tearful good-byes? Come on, Eth, give us a good quote."

"No ceremony," Ethan said briefly. Was it Elizabeth's imagination, or was he shivering slightly? "Just—just get it over with."

Elizabeth bit her lip. "Remember what Hatta would say," she said, suppressing a giggle. "Now, we don't stand on ceremony here!" she said in their hostess's voice.

Jessica smiled weakly. Then, with all her might, she flung the pot to the stones at her feet. There was a sudden smashing noise that seemed to tear through Elizabeth's heart—and then there was silence. The pot lay on the ground, a thousand tiny pieces mixed into the mud of the riverbank.

"Wow," Jessica said as if to herself. "I didn't—I didn't think I'd thrown it that hard."

Gentle waves lapped against the shore. Elizabeth rubbed her eyes. The pieces weren't actually burrowing their way back into the ground, were they? She blinked once, twice, three times.

It almost—looked that way.

"'Home is the sailor, home from the sea,'" Ethan murmured by her side. He reached for Elizabeth's hand and held it. "Robert Louis Stevenson."

"So it's gone." Jessica straightened up, her

mouth a tight line. "I created the pot, and now I've destroyed it. And I sure hope Hatta is right." She looked unhappily at the shards of pot lying scattered among the stones.

"Weird," Bernard said uneasily. "I've never seen a pot smash like that. And I've seen a bunch smashed up, believe you me. It's almost like—like it wanted . . ." His voice trailed off.

"Listen." Elizabeth cupped her free hand to her ear. "What's that sound?" She listened intently. "It sounds like—like a paddle. And like somebody singing."

"It's coming from under the bridge." Bernard pointed.

Elizabeth followed his finger. A second passed, then two, and then, like an arrow, a canoe shot into view—a silvery gray aluminum boat with Nature Scouts, USA inscribed on the front.

"Oh man." Jessica clapped her hand to her mouth.

Elizabeth gasped. She stared first at the tiny remnants of Jessica's curse pot, lying at her feet in the mud from which it had come—and then at Susan Rainer, very much alive and paddling along in the front of the canoe.

Fifteen

◇

"So I've figured it all out," Marion said happily. The twins had just walked into Woodbridge Hall after their trip to see Hatta, and Marion had met them at the door. "The world's greatest detective lives! No autographs please," she added modestly.

Jessica poked Elizabeth. "What's she talking about?" she asked.

"Susan's disappearance, you bozo," Marion answered. "The detective that never sleeps, that's me. Well, I made some discreet inquiries, and I found out some interesting stuff." She whipped out a notebook. "First, I located Susan's professor in the class she was taking, and he verified that she hadn't been to class since Monday. Then I went, in disguise of course, to the class and asked around, and—"

"Get to the point, please," Jessica said, faking a yawn.

"Anyway," Marion went on, "I put two and two together and went to find Mike, remember Mike? Only surprise! no Mike. It wasn't easy to find him without a last name or anything, but I did it," she added, looking pleased. "Turns out he's a Nature Scout, did you know that? And the Nature Scouts—"

"—left to go canoeing on the day Susan disappeared," Jessica supplied, giving Marion a tolerant smile. How could she have forgotten that Mike was a Nature Scout? It was about the only thing he'd told her before Susan came along and stole him.

"Right," Marion agreed grudgingly. "So, anyway, I put two and two together, and I'm positive that Susan passed herself off as a Nature Scout and went on the canoeing trip too." She leaned against the wall, a pleased look in her eyes. "Q. E. D. That's what you say when you prove something."

"Ah," Jessica said, nudging Elizabeth. "Very clever, Marion. There's only one problem." She waited a beat. "You're wrong."

"We reversed the curse," Elizabeth explained. "Jessica returned the pot to the clay where it had come from, and poof! Susan appeared."

"Yeah, it was so cool," Jessica agreed. She draped her arm around Elizabeth and gestured off into the distance. "And, look, here comes Susan now." She could see her roommate beginning to climb up the steps toward the dormitory.

Marion turned around.

"It's amazing what a little curse reversal can do," Jessica said brightly. "I threw it into the clay, said a few magic words, and—" She shrugged. "Instant Susan."

"Whoa!" Marion licked her lips and turned to the twins. "You're not, like, serious, are you?" she blurted out. "You couldn't have—*could you?*"

"Like I said." Jessica snapped her fingers.

"Poof," Elizabeth said.

Marion stared at Susan. "It sure looks like her," she began. "Wait a minute—" She frowned. "OK, I've got it now," she said. "Very funny, nice try, and all that. When you brought the pot back to smash— and I'm assuming you really did smash it—you took it to a river, right?"

Jessica wrinkled her nose. "Um—yeah," she admitted.

"And after you broke it, there was this canoe that came into sight," Marion went on. She began to grin. "On that very same river. And the canoe probably said National Nature Scouts on the side—"

"Nature Scouts, USA," Elizabeth corrected her.

"And she was in one seat," Marion continued, jabbing a finger at Susan, "and he was in the other. Am I right?" She jerked her thumb toward Mike, in a Nature Scouts uniform, who was struggling up the hill behind Susan.

"Right," the twins admitted in one breath.

"Like I said," Marion said coolly. "Never try to fool a great detective." She stepped aside as Susan approached. "Hey, Susan," she called out. "Have a nice trip?"

Susan just rolled her eyes. "You'd better not have messed with my stuff," she said to Jessica, banging the door behind her.

Jessica sighed. "Too bad the curse pot didn't change her personality."

The student union building still looked like a grounded battleship, Elizabeth decided, but the basement was quite a nice place with all the decorations hanging up. It was Friday evening, and there was a dance going on for all the summer program students and faculty.

"May I have this dance?" Ethan asked. He held out his hand to Elizabeth.

Elizabeth giggled. "Charmed," she said, and they moved together onto the dance floor.

The music was wild and crazy, and lights were flashing everywhere. In the distance Elizabeth could see Jessica and Bernard dancing away. "Are all the dances crowded as this?" she yelled over the din of the music.

"Worse!" Ethan screamed back happily.

He was a surprisingly good dancer for such a serious guy, Elizabeth thought, watching him. She really, really liked him. He was smart and funny and sweet. Plus, he was cute. And he was nice to her. She thought back to the poems he'd written her and how good they'd made her feel . . .

But there was a lump in her throat she couldn't quite shake.

"Ethan?" she asked when the music had ended. "Could we, like, get a Coke and talk somewhere?"

"Sure!" Ethan pushed his hair off his forehead.

Elizabeth decided not to tell him until after they'd sat down at a table far from the dance floor. "It's about—us, Ethan," she said nervously, toying with her glass. "It's—it's our ages." How could she tell him, in a nice way, that he was too old for her? she wondered. When she'd first discovered that Ethan was really just sixteen, she'd been thrilled. But now that she thought about it, four years, even three and a half, was a pretty big age difference. "It's, it's just that—"

"That I'm really a little too old for you," Ethan supplied. His eyes were smiling. "That's what you were going to say, wasn't it?"

Elizabeth nodded. "I hope you're not—upset."

Ethan shrugged. "Of course I'm upset," he said. "Who wouldn't be? But, you know, I was thinking the same thing. Four years is kind of a lot at our age." He took a quick sip of his drink. "But I figure we can go ahead and dance anyway."

"Oh of course we can!" Elizabeth was surprised. "I—I really like you a lot, Ethan," she stammered. "I don't, um, want you to take this the wrong way."

"I don't take it the wrong way," Ethan said. "I like you a lot too, Elizabeth. In fact, here's what I'd like to suggest. Tonight, we'll dance together. And next week, we'll enjoy each other's company in class and maybe at lunch a couple of times." He grinned at Elizabeth. "OK?"

"OK," Elizabeth agreed cautiously. "And then?"

Ethan shrugged. "And then we go our separate ways. But I'll keep having a crush on you, and maybe you'll have a crush on me too."

Elizabeth's eyes sparkled. "Maybe," she said.

"And in a few years, who knows?" Ethan ran his fingers through his hair and smiled his toothy grin. "When you're sixteen and I'm twenty—or when you're twenty and I'm twenty-four . . ."

"Yeah." Elizabeth looked up and smiled. Anything could happen. She sighed. "That sounds good, Ethan. So this won't be, like, good-bye forever."

"No way." Ethan sounded contemptuous. "Do you remember the poem I quoted to you on the bridge that night—the night we first met?" he asked.

How could I forget? Elizabeth thought, but she raised her eyebrows and said, "Remind me."

Ethan rubbed his chin. "I think it still fits. It's by Longfellow. From 'The Arrow and the Song'?" In a husky voice, he began to recite, and Elizabeth joined in.

"'And the song, from beginning to end,'" they

said together, reaching for each other's hand, "'I found in the heart of a friend.'"

"So what were you and Ethan talking about so seriously over there?" Jessica wanted to know.

"Yeah, what?" Marion chimed in.

Elizabeth smiled a shy smile. "Well—we were talking about breaking up."

"Breaking up?" Jessica looked indignant. "But you're not even together yet!"

"I thought you liked him," Marion said. "And he likes you too. It doesn't take a detective to figure that out."

"We do like each other," Elizabeth said. "A lot. But he's too old for me, and so . . . we'll just have a crush on each other until we're old enough to decide what we really want to do." She blushed a little. "I guess . . . I guess that sounds pretty silly, huh?"

"Yeah, it sounds silly all right," Jessica agreed. "But also kind of romantic . . ."

SWEET VALLEY TWINS

Created by Francine Pascal

Have you read the latest titles in the Sweet Valley Twins series?
Ask your bookseller for any you may have missed:

TWINS IN LOVE
THE MYSTERIOUS DR Q
ELIZABETH SOLVES IT ALL
BIG BROTHER'S IN LOVE AGAIN
JESSICA'S LUCKY MILLIONS
BREAKFAST OF ENEMIES
THE TWINS HIT HOLLYWOOD
CAMMI'S CRUSH

SWEET VALLEY HIGH™

Created by Francine Pascal

The top-selling teenage series starring identical twins Jessica and Elizabeth Wakefield and all their friends at Sweet Valley High. One new title every month!

Recent titles:

THE SADDLE CLUB

by Bonnie Bryant

Saddle up and ride free with Stevie, Carole and Lisa. These three very different girls come together to share their special love of horses and to create The Saddle Club. Don't miss the latest titles in this super series:

We hope you enjoyed reading this book.

All Sweet Valley Twins™ books are available by post from:

Bookservice by Post, PO Box 29,
Douglas, Isle of Man IM99 1BQ

Credit Cards accepted.
Please telephone 01624 675137,
fax 01624 670923
or Internet http://www.bookpost.co.uk
or e-mail: bookshop@enterprise.net for details.

Free postage and packing in the UK.
Overseas customers allow £1 per book (paperbacks)
and £3 per book (hardbacks)